SPECIAL MESSAGE TO READERS

This book is published under the auspices of

THE ULVERSCROFT FOUNDATION

(registered charity No. 264873 UK)

Established in 1972 to provide funds for research, diagnosis and treatment of eye diseases. Examples of contributions made are: —

A Children's Assessment Unit at Moorfield's Hospital, London.

•

Twin operating theatres at the Western Ophthalmic Hospital, London.

•

A Chair of Ophthalmology at the Royal Australian College of Ophthalmologists.

•

The Ulverscroft Children's Eye Unit at the Great Ormond Street Hospital For Sick Children London.

You can help further the work of the Foundation by making a donation or leaving a legacy. Every contribution, no matter how small, is received with gratitude. Please write for details to:

THE ULVERSCROFT FOUNDATION,
The Green, Bradgate Road, Anstey,
Leicester LE7 7FU, England.
Telephone: (0116) 236 4325

In Australia write to:

THE ULVERSCROFT FOUNDATION,
c/o The Royal Australian and New Zealand College of Ophthalmologists,
94-98, Chalmers Street, Surry Hills,
N.S.W. 2010, Australia

LYNCH'S LAW

Pat Lynch, ex-Clydeside hard man, ex-Mayfair snooper, emerges from prison to find he has a client — a dead one. Richard Scott has bequeathed him his modest savings, and a last request — that he discover who had murdered his daughter two years earlier. The case is old, cold and hopeless, but Lynch is touched by the dead man's faith that he can succeed where the police have given up. Lynch re-opens it, and a chance remark by a friend of the murdered girl blazes a new trail, which he follows to the Midlands . . .

JAMES BALNAVE

LYNCH'S LAW

Complete and Unabridged

LINFORD
Leicester

First published in Great Britain in 1980 by
Robert Hale Limited
London

First Linford Edition
published 2005
by arrangement with
Robert Hale Limited
London

British Library CIP Data

Balnave, James
Lynch's law.—Large print ed.—
Linford mystery library
1. Detective and mystery stories
2. Large type books
I. Title
823.9′14 [F]

ISBN 1–84395–822–8

Published by
F. A. Thorpe (Publishing)
Anstey, Leicestershire

Set by Words & Graphics Ltd.
Anstey, Leicestershire
Printed and bound in Great Britain by
T. J. International Ltd., Padstow, Cornwall

This book is printed on acid-free paper

1

Through the open top of the sash window Lynch could hear the orchestration of gears on Peckham Rye, the tinkling laugh of a girl outside in the decrepit square, the firing squad burst as her boy friend kicked his machine into life. 'Summer in Camberwell' muttered Lynch, as he settled his aching body deeper into the arthritic mattress.

The roar swelled to an unbearable thunder and Lynch jumped from the bed with an oath and threw up the window. The machine pencilled a wide arch in the melting tarmac and flashed under his eyes. He had a quick take of the pillion rider's long leg, bare from sandal to thigh, white and unashamedly beautiful, then it was gone, motor bike and riders. But the after image of young flaunted limb remained; two years of enforced continence can be tricky to handle.

'Maybe I should buy me a motor cycle,'

thought Lynch as he turned away from the window, 'find out what makes the aphrodisiac — the noise or the speed.'

He was wide awake now. His watch showed half past seven. He looked with a shudder round his dingy bed-sitter: it looked like an old man's dirty vest. In the Old Kent Road the Friday night tide of shapeless mums would be sweeping with remorseless jollity towards Bingo; the dance halls and discos would be opening their doors; the first pints of bitter would be cascading down dockers' throats. Who wanted to moulder the evening away in a ten pound a week tomb? Not Lynch.

From the sagging wardrobe he took out his one suit and laid it out on the bed; its Savile Row elegance made the room blush. The scabrous mirror showed a blue black bristle on his bony Hebridean face, and a peppering of gray.

'You are forty-four', he reminded his sour reflection, 'not a callant any longer.'

It would have to be a closer than close shave.

He filled the kettle from the cracked wash basin in the corner, shed his sweat-stained shirt, and began stropping the cut throat razor on the old L.M.S. window strap; unwittingly his hand fell into the rhythm of a Highland tramping song, and Lynch realised that for the first time in two years he was whistling.

'That's what 'A glimpse of stocking' does for you,' he told himself. 'Tells you you're not dead.'

Except that she wasn't wearing stockings. Possibly there were other things she was not wearing, which, he told himself very firmly, were not the concern of a prurient middle-aged ex-con.

The shining blade froze on the up-stroke; the knock on his door came again, louder this time, peremptory. Two silent steps took him back to the window. The square decayed emptily in the evening sun. But not totally void. A well groomed Rover 3500 stood outside the front door. Solidly opulent, not flashy. It hadn't been there a few moments ago.

There was nobody in it.

His eyes probed the peeling walls, the shadowed doorways, the blank-eyed windows.

Nobody.

A child screeched angrily in another street.

Lynch slid up the top of the window, latched it tight. Always protect your rear, especially if it's on the ground floor.

He moved over and stood behind the locked door, a little to one side.

'Who is it?' he asked quietly, moving another step aside the instant the words were uttered. Always protect your front, too.

'My name is Price-Carruthers,' came the voice from the other side of the door, 'and I should be grateful if I could have a word with you.'

The hyphen in the name had percolated strength nine through the wooden panel, but Lynch made no move.

'Would I be grateful if you had a word with me, Price-Carruthers?'

It was unlikely that Strapper had now got round to using muscle with double barrelled names, Public School accents, and establishment cars, but you could never tell: progress was all around you.

'Oh, I think so.' The well-bred voice

had a slight head of hauteur, by now. 'You may hear something to your advantage.'

You didn't hear the report of the shot that took you between the eyes, which some people thought was a blessing, though Lynch was not one of them. He was having morbid thoughts again; he'd have to watch that.

The oil-filmed bolt he had fixed whispered in his hand as he slid it back, flattening himself against the wall in the same instant.

'You don't need a penny,' he called. 'Just turn the handle and walk in.'

The door opened away from Lynch and to his left. Price-Carruthers' pin-striped leg took one step across the threshold and stopped.

Lynch, watching the tableau in the cracked wardrobe mirror, facing the doorway did not blame the leg one little bit. The doorway framed Price-Carruthers in the regimentals of the City-dark suit, bowler, wash leather gloves, umbrella in the crook of the left arm. On his right, another figure in scuffed flannel trousers, a string vest sprouting black hair, and a lethal open razor at the high port — himself, Lynch. If the leg had any sense it would withdraw itself sharply and try the Athenaeum. 'You catch me at my toilet,' said Lynch, dropping his arm; there was no one behind Price-Carruthers.

'Come in, take a chair, take the chair.'

Price-Carruthers came in, twitching his nostrils only slightly; he was determined not to find the situation distasteful. He took his determination over to the jagged wickerwork chair and bravely sat on the twigs. Lynch leaned against the door, pushed the bolt home with his free hand and studied his visitor.

The fair hair with the discreet wave was barbered weekly, the scrubbed pink cheeks advertised the best after-shave and a daily quota of gin, the weekly squash game would hold the well washed, well-fed flesh as far as the late thirties, and they were just round the corner.

'What is it?' asked Lynch lathering his chin, 'washing machines, tooled leather encyclopedias to get me past the 11+, deodorants. Whatever it is I need it.'

'I am not a salesman.' The ice was falling off his voice in great shards. 'I am a solicitor — Hawtrey, Mongan and Price-Carruthers.'

'You make it sound like a Papal Bull,' grunted Lynch, scraping his jaw bone. 'Now can I hear something to my advantage?'

'Are you Patrick Aloysius Cameron Lynch?'

'God save Lochiel and the king over the water, I am.'

'Born in Glasgow on the 4th of April, 1933?'

'No. Born in Govan on the 4th of April, 1933.'

'There is a distinction?'

Lynch wiped his face clean on a snow white towel.

'There are places I know where they will prove it with a broken bottle in your face, but is hardly germane, and it is doubtful if it was to my advantage.' He stripped down to the buff and put his soiled underwear in a laundry bag, then he padded over to the drawers to find fresh clothes. From the strain on

Price-Carruther's face he deduced that this was not the norm in Lincoln's Inn Fields.

'My information is that you joined the Cameronians as a private in 1951, transferred to the Marine Commandos as a sergeant in 1953, were commissioned in the Parachute Regiment in 1955 — ' the recital limped a little at this point, 'did intelligence work in Germany in the sixties, a stint with the S.A.S. and then there was a disagreement with an American three star general.'

'Linguistic misunderstanding really,' explained Lynch sadly, 'I called him a big steaming shite. He assumed I was labelling him a member of the Iranian political party and he was a bit upset. I told him it was a Lowland variant of a much loved Anglo-Saxon pejorative, but he wouldn't be consoled — prickly sort of chap.'

'So you resigned in 1973 — as a major — with a D.S.O.?'

Even though he was reading from his own notes, the lawyer's incredulity at this last bit floated round the room like a luminous balloon.

'Accurate but incomplete,' said Lynch, buttoning up his crisply laundered shirt, 'you skipped over the best bits.'

'Such as?'

'Oh, the Court Martial in 1952 for kicking a Provost Marshal in the crotch on the Waverley Steps, the affair with the Guards' Colonel's wife in Malta, the Donnybrook in Worms on Hogmanay — the highlights of my military service, you might say.'

'I imagine there are a number of salient points about you we may not have been apprised of.'

One up for the Inner Temple, thought Lynch.

'When you — er — left the Army you set up your own Inquiry Agency in Mayfair.'

'No agency — just me. I had my little private eye at some of the most ornate keyholes in Belgravia.'

'One gathers that it was a lucrative business and not without colour.'

Lynch selected the best known from his collection of Public School ties and watched his guest wince.

'I ate my fish and chips in the privacy of my own Bentley, if that's what you mean.'

'Two years ago you were sentenced at the Old Bailey for inflicting grevious bodily harm on Josef Strapper described as a Soho club owner.'

Lynch sat on the bed facing his visitor and pulled on his trousers. When he spoke his voice was low and grave, like a little wind out of Siberia.

'I served my full time, I was not a good boy, I don't know how to be. Two weeks ago I was spewed back into Society and I got a job as a navvy on the new Motorway; I also took up residence in these desirable chambers. Tonight, for the first time in two years, I am going out for the evening. I shall dine at a good restaurant, drink good brandy, look at the naked shoulders of beautiful scented women, be where the living is easy, do the town. You, Price-bloody-Carruthers are delaying me, not diverting me. What the hell do you want?'

The lawyer's Adam's apple oscillated

rapidly over his tight collar.

'Josef Strapper nearly died, the papers said, he was months in hospital, and now he walks with a stick.'

Lynch pulled on gossamer thin black socks and eased his feet into his 'working shoes' — gleaming leather, masking steel toe-caps: you never knew in the West End. 'If I had wanted to kill Strapper he would be dead. Why don't you get to the meat, I've had all the vegetables?'

'The day after you were sentenced a girl was shot dead on the common at Englefield Green. She was twenty-seven years old and she worked as a typist at an Estate Agent's in Staines High Street. The day, you will remember, was a Thursday — the fourteenth of May. It was sunny but there was a fair breeze — '

'The breeze is important?'

'You will see why,' Price-Carruthers assured him.

'The police reconstructed her movements with some care. She left the office at half past four which was her usual time on a Thursday. She boarded a bus at her usual stop by Staines Bridge at her usual time, twenty to five, and at ten to five she started to walk across the Green as she usually did. The German au pair who exercised her mistress's poodle every afternoon at around the same time bade her 'Good Evening'.'

'Which she usually did,' interrupted Lynch.

'Frequently, anyway. At about six minutes to five there was one shot and two people saw the girl, Valerie Scott, fall.'

'The German maid — '

'And a fourteen year old schoolboy, Robert Wilkie, who was also on his way home across the green. Both witnesses reached her at the same time. She was dead.

'Wilkie, for his age, behaved with coolness and sense. He stayed with the body and sent Miss Schmidt to the nearest house to telephone for ambulance and police. While he waited for help to come he used his eyes, as he put it, to see whether he could 'spot anything suspicious'. He didn't, nor did anyone else. By five past five the police were on the scene and the investigation was under way. The post-mortem showed that Valerie Scott had been killed by a .303 rifle bullet through the left ventricle of the heart. The police worked out that the shot had been fired from a little copse in front of Miss Scott and to the right of the axis of her route. The distance from the firing point to the body was one hundred and eighty nine yards, two feet, and the breeze, which I mentioned earlier, was blowing from left to right across her path at fifteen miles an hour.'

'Telescopic sight,' mused Lynch, 'but still a tricky sort of shot at a bad angle at a moving target.'

'Valerie was wearing, as it happened, a piece of sparkling costume jewellery, on her left breast. That must have helped the rifleman.'

'It's still competent marksmanship.'

'The fact should have pointed a finger to someone connected with Valerie Scott. It didn't. She had no current or past boyfriends who had any discoverable acquaintanceship with rifle shooting, or any other kind of shooting for that matter.'

‘A hiring and firing?’

‘A murderer and a marksman? Not easy to find, and the price would be steep. And that postulates a very good motive. The police couldn’t find one. The active enquiry went on for a month and was quietly shelved; there was nothing more for the police to do.’

Lynch contemplated his face in a lambent toe-cap.

‘Theories?’

Price-Carruthers eased himself from one set of splinters on to another, and, for a moment, Lynch contemplated offering him a drink but the idea of pure malt wasted on a gin and bitters palate shocked him; anyway, he didn’t have much left. He sat where he was.

‘There seemed only two possibilities — accident, which was discarded — and random malice, which wasn’t.’

‘Murder for pleasure? That could become a habit.’

‘It hasn’t, not in two years.’

‘The devotee could have moved, or died, or taken up macramé.’

‘Maybe. Speculation is unfettered.’

Through the window Lynch could see the shadows creeping up the flayed façade across the way. A boy on a bicycle slalomed one-handed down the street and the guitars from his transistor pounded, and ebbed. In the West End dark jowled Levantines would be pouring champagne with the reverence of monks at vespers, and theatre audiences would be settling contentedly into red plush.

'What's in it for me?'

Price-Carruthers sat up straighter and the chair creaked like an old ship's mast.

'Valerie Scott lived with her widowed father who was a retired minor Civil Servant. They had no relations. Eighteen months ago he came into our Staines office to make a will. He was already ailing when his daughter was killed, and, when I saw him, it was obvious he was a very sick man. He died a month after he signed the will. It is rather an unusual will but simple, and perfectly legal. I have it at my Staines office and you can see it there whenever you wish.'

'Haud oan a minit, Jimmie, haud oan! Whenever I wish? Why should I wish? I am not a collector of testamentary bric-a-brac.'

'Because you are the sole legatee. Richard Scott, as you would expect, was not a rich man; he had been the tenant of the same small semi-detached house for . . . '

'Wait! Say that first bit again about me being the sole whatsit!'

The lawyer tutted impatiently, 'Legatee. It's not such an abstruse term as to be totally unfamiliar to the lay mind. The net value of the estate comes to — '

'Never mind the net value, Buzzfuzz, or even the gross, for a second. So far as I know, my last remaining relative fell into the Clyde at the Broomielaw while in a catatonic trance induced by a pint of raw methylated spirit. That was ten years ago and nobody has seen him since. Besides, his name was McGarrity. And the only Civil Servants I've had anything to do with recently have been members of Her Majesty's Prison Service and they weren't very fraternal.'

'Mr Scott had never met you but he read about you in the papers and what he read seemed to impress him in some way — '

'But not you?'

The other shook his head firmly and went on.

'When he made his wishes known to me at our first meeting I pointed out that lurid pen pictures in the popular press are seldom a good basis for the disposal of one's property. He agreed to wait for a fortnight while I tried to find out a little more about you.'

'Two minutes in a Park Lane bistro would have been enough. What did you sweep up, little gleaner?'

The pink face deepened to dark red.

'I reported to my client that you were a private inquiry agent with little regard for the law, or its agents; profligate in women, whisky and cards; unmanageable; violent — ferociously so at times; an adherent to your own esoteric sense of justice, whatever it is; and never known to be dishonest. I hope I did you fair.'

'Oh proud, old lad, proud, especially that last bit. You could not say I was honest just 'never known to be dishonest'

— there's a jurisprudential quiddity if ever I heard one. So what was your client's reaction to your little vignette?'

'He still insisted on drawing up the same will though I advised strongly against it. In the end I drew it up. The terms of it, briefly, are that as soon as you were released from jail I was to hand over the cash realised from the estate. It amounts to two thousand, three hundred and forty-seven pounds.'

'Why? Why me?'

'He left a letter for you which I am to hand over to you with the money. That is also at my Staines office, but the gist of it I know: he hoped you would use the money to find out why his daughter was killed, and to bring his daughter's murderer to whatever justice you thought fit.'

'That was not a condition?'

'Oh no. You inherit quite unconditionally; the testator expressed a wish, he did not impose an obligation.'

Lynch crossed to the battered chest of drawers for his silver backed hair brushes.

'I bet you made that abundantly clear

— about not imposing a condition.'

'I advised my client to the best of my ability.'

He attacked his black thatch with angry blows.

'And rightly so, Price-Carruthers. So — there's nothing to stop me pocketing the old boy's life savings and then forgetting that he or his daughter ever existed.'

'Nothing.'

'Only my — what did you call it? 'esoteric sense of justice' whatever the hell that is. How and when do I collect the loot?'

The lawyer stood up and handed Lynch a card.

'Be at my office in Staines on Monday morning at ten o'clock with proof of identity and we can conclude the transaction.'

Monday could not come too quickly for him.

'Proof of identity?'

'Birth Certificate, passport, something like that.'

'A reference from my last employer?'

'A mere formality of documentation. I have no doubt that you are Patrick Aloysius Cameron Lynch. Good evening.'

He swept out of the room with all the dignity of a dowager duchess.

From the window Lynch watched him climb into the immaculate Rover which gathered its skirts from the squalor around it and picked its way daintily out of the square.

He turned back into the room and poured a large unmeasured Malt. One should never be hasty, he reflected; a pompous twit to whom Lynch would have given ten cable lengths of sea room in a flat calm turns out to be Santa Claus in civvies, a reluctant and patronising one, but still — .

He turned and lifted his glass to the smeared window. 'To Price and Carruthers,' he toasted aloud, 'may you never be separated.'

It was turning out to be not such a bad evening after all.

2

Staines at ten o'clock on Monday morning had the relaxed air of a wife who's just got her husband off to work and kids off to school. As Lynch came down the High Street from the station the young sun gentled him, the first shoppers were moving, unhurried, along the pavement, the delivery vans were burrowing, as usual, for parking spaces, but good naturedly. He put his scuffed leather bag down and leisurely filled his meerschaum with the Dunhill mixture he had expansively bought that morning. For the first time in two years he felt relaxed: Camberwell, Brixton, were an old dream — fading.

Price-Carruthers had the floor over a grocer's. Four windows carried, in large gilt letters the emblem: 'Hawtrey, Mongan & Price-Carruthers, Solicitors and Commissioners for Oaths'; they were large windows — they had to be. The blonde typist who slid open the glass panel at his knock had a landscaped bosom and an expectant pout.

'Ye-es?'

Someday her hero was going to bounce straight out of the television screen and stand in front of her faerie casement, but not today it seemed.

'Lynch. To see Mr Price-Carruthers.'

'The door on your right. He's expecting you.'

The glass panel closed abruptly.

The lawyer was in pale authority behind a wide modern desk.

'Good morning. You are on time.'

'Like Pavlov's dogs. Somebody waves a pound note, I salivate.'

One by one, Lynch placed the documents on the strawberry pink blotting pad.

'Birth Certificate — Army Discharge Papers — Driving Licence — P.45 — Passport — Income Tax Demand. Pat Lynch! This is your life!'

Price-Carruthers gazed at him, stonily, for a moment, then bent himself to the task of examining the papers in front of him, carefully, scrupulously.

'Quite conclusive,' he said, handing them back in a neat bundle. 'The cheque is already made out. I left it open: I didn't know whether you had a bank account or not.'

Lynch took it and looked at it.

'Local bank?'

'It's just a little way down the High Street. I'll go down with you, if you want to present it immediately, so there won't be any difficulty. Banks are rather careful about large open cheques.'

'Civil of you: I'll take you up on that.'

'This is Scott's letter to you and in this file is all the information on Valerie Scott that I could gather. I'm afraid it is pretty thin. In fact it won't tell you much more than I did last Friday, but it has dates, addresses, newspaper cuttings, report of the inquest.'

Lynch stared at him. 'I thought you said there were no conditions?'

Price-Carruthers flushed. 'Neither there are; but there's the file, just in case you become interested.'

Lynch flipped it open cursorily.

'Inspector Gibb and Superintendent Matthews? Even if I tried to become interested I'd have to get along without the co-operation of the police.'

'You know them? They struck me as efficient.'

'Oh, they are. They have a record of arrests and convictions stretching from Pentonville to Parkhurst, and they like adding to it, but they don't like me. Anyway if they found nothing there is nothing to find.'

'Perhaps if you talked to them — '

'If I was a blind man trying to cross the road on a dark foggy night they wouldn't tell me where the pedestrian crossing was. They'd charge me with importuning.'

He folded the file and slipped it into his inside pocket with the letter. He signed the receipt the lawyer pushed across to him.

'Gibb and Matthews apart, who could one talk to about Valerie Scott?'

'She had a very good friend, a schoolmistress called Frances Gavin who has a cottage in Datchet, the address is in the file. They were very close though you wouldn't have expected it.'

'Why not?'

'Of course I never met either of them but Valerie Scott was just a typist and this girl Gavin has a degree from Oxford and teaches Physics in a rather good girls' school. You know what I mean.'

'The class barriers are falling one by one, sonny; you'd better watch your head.'

'Shall we go to the bank?' said Price-Carruthers, tightly.

'With all dispatch,' said Lynch, making for the door.

'Don't forget your bag.'

'That would never do,' said Lynch, hefting it up, 'I might have to come back for it.'

They emerged blinking into the sun washed street and set off in the direction of the river. Beyond Staines Bridge the gasometer heaved its squat conic ugliness into the azure sky.

Lynch glanced at his companion and had a sudden picture of a scarlet procession of judges with their posies warding away the malodrous centuries. Price-Carruthers' ambulant aloofness was a posy against all the dirty necked Lynches of the universe. He would make a fine judge, Lynch reflected, a hanging judge.

'That is the Estate Agent's where she worked — Valerie Scott I mean.'

It had taken Lynch weeks to achieve the old lag's ventriloquial habit of speaking without moving your head or your lips, and here was a lawyer with all the skill of a lifer.

'Trott, Chudleigh and Co.' had windows full of desirable residences in exchange for only one's life's blood.

They entered the cool filtered shade of the bank in silence and Price-Carruthers knocked at the manager's door without preamble.

'Ah, Fullerton,' he greeted the man who opened the door, 'this is the *CLIENT* I rang you about, the one with the open cheque.'

The bank manager was a slight middle-aged man with faded blue eyes which focussed stonily on the lawyer. Lynch wondered how often only Head Office had stood between Price-Carruthers and a mouthful of cancelled cheques.

Fullerton turned his back on him and gave his hand to Lynch.

'I'll look after Mr Lynch,' he said over his shoulder, 'there's no need to keep you from your office.'

He ushered Lynch into an airy, green carpeted room and shut the door firmly in his escort's face.

'Fullerton, my lad,' said Lynch, 'you are a bank manager I could learn to love.'

* * *

An hour later Lynch was nosing the red Sunbeam Alpine into the stream of traffic crossing the bridge to the Surrey bank.

'Go to O'Leary,' Fullerton had told him, 'and mention my name. O'Leary loves cars more than he loves money and that's saying a lot. He'll want two hundred pounds for four week's hire, and he'll take a hundred and sixty if he thinks you'll look after it; but only a sports car, mind you, he doesn't care about the others.'

And so it had turned out.

On the seat beside him rested his old leather bag and the new pig-skin hold-all, containing the clothes that had covered him thirty minutes before. Apart from the shoes, everything he was now wearing was new — ready made, true, but the best Staines could offer in a hurry — cavalry twill slacks, gleaming white shirt, Rifle Brigade throat scarf.

From the whirlpool of the roundabout he shot into the A30 and saw the long stretch of road curving gently round Strodes playing fields. This was as good a place to find out whether O'Leary was as good as his myth.

He put his foot down; the car under him whipped forward like a greyhound out of the trap; the line of poplars on his left coalesced in a rippling green blur; the needle jumped to eighty and held; and the Egham roundabout rushed towards him growing fast. He held his speed overlong — deliberately — then stamped down on the brake hard. The car reared on its haunches, protesting, but holding true to its axis. He slipped sedately behind a gravel lorry and took the roundabout at a walk. O'Leary's merchandise was even better than the commercial. The car would do, it would most certainly do.

Traffic was fast and light and he was on the long glide down into Virginia Water before he expected it. Half way down he found his turning — a serpentine alley of a B road, conga-ing through woods vibrant with dappled light and pealing with birdsong. A mile along and he turned onto a drive which shouldered between massive stone pillars to girdle a long, low, two storeyed building of Cotswold stone, which glowed warm in the sun. Sprinklers shimmered lazily over emerald lawns and a peacock strode through regally, its plumage glistening with diamonds. Lynch took his bags out of the car and ascended wide worn steps to a massive doorway over which was poised, slightly off-centre, an eroded stone shield. This was the hotel's only sign: it paid 'The Crusader' not to advertise. He put the bags down on a high-backed settee in the empty reception lobby and followed the lighted arrow to the bar.

Rich dark panelling muted the well bred conversation which faltered, almost imperceptibly, then resumed as the Rifle Brigade cravat was noted and filed. The men's directorships sat on them with the same ease as the Dior frocks caressed their women. The air was a collage of cigar smoke, Chanel, and warmed brandy.

Lynch zigzagged through the miniature refectory tables to the long gleaming bar counter where a square, white-jacketed, elderly emperor dispensed justice. As he came up the barman reached under the counter, brought up a nearly full bottle of Glenlivet and poured two measures: a single in one glass, a generous treble in the other. He pushed the larger one over to Lynch.

'Slainte!'

'Slainte!' replied Lynch.

They drank slowly in companionable silence.

'Welcome back, sir. It's been two years at least.'

'No remission,' said Lynch.

'The winter months weren't much here anyway. Damp.'

Lynch's empty glass was filled. 'You'll be staying?'

'A few days, a week or so. I may be in and out. You know how it is, Charles. Providing you have room for me, of course.'

Charles's raised eyebrows were eloquent, 'There's always room for you. Will you be alone this time?'

'For the beginning, at any rate, but you never know what'll come up.'

'No, sir, you never know. You can have the Marchioness room, as usual. I'll get Biddy to move the Swiss couple out; she's a pig anyway.'

Biddy was the Management? Owner? Co-owner with Charles. Lynch didn't know, and had no intention of asking, ever.

'I've already put it in train,' boomed a voice behind Lynch's right ear, and a large hand gripped his shoulder like an affectionate steel clamp, 'I recognised that old leather bag in the lobby.'

Biddy was six feet two in her nylons,

with the torso of a heavy-weight in training, and more feminine charm than a Ziegfield chorus.

He took the hand from his shoulder and kissed it lingeringly.

'Biddy, I've missed you.'

'Was it bad? Brixton I mean.'

'Not good. Their housekeeping is a long way behind yours. They don't have your high regard for bed linen.'

'Chump! There's a rump steak for your lunch and the Beaujolais is on me.'

She sailed off with all the grace of a transatlantic liner.

3

It was just after three when he recrossed Staines Bridge. A schoolboy eight was thrusting a slim racing shell up river with perspiring elan, and a squadron of swans wheeled and turned in review. He found a parking place by the old Staines West station and walked back to the High Street and 'Trott, Chudleigh & Co.' who turned out, not unnaturally, to be conjoined in the singular person of Mr Bundy.

'There hasn't been a Trott in the firm for forty years, but of course we keep the name,' explained Bundy.

'Of course,' agreed Lynch.

He didn't ask about Chudleigh.

The walls of the estate agent's private sanctum were blazoned with calendars from Building Societies, Insurance Companies, and Builders; Bundy would always know what day it was. Here and there were tinted photographs of suburban detached and semis. Two king sized framed certificates proclaimed Bundy's membership of whatever Estate Agents belonged to. In neat grey suiting, bow tie, Rotary badge, and horn rims, Bundy enunciated the middle aged middleman, dripping with probity.

'Valerie Scott?' he repeated. 'Tragic. We sent a large wreath. Naturally I went to the funeral.'

No one would ever catch Bundy not doing the correct thing.

'Naturally. I wonder whether you could tell me anything about her?'

Bundy's eyes glittered behind the horn rims, 'Why? You're not police, are you?'

Lynch shook his head. 'Let us just say a friend of the family, though I never met Valerie. I've been away for over two years. I'm curious.'

Bundy nodded his understanding, 'Not a lot to tell. I suppose I'm the only one here now who knew her. You've no idea what the staff turnover's like these days. They no sooner take the covers off the typewriters than they're engaged or they want to work up in town. 'You won't be any better off,' I tell them, 'the travelling will get you down.' But will they listen? I took one on three weeks ago, straight out of school at twenty pounds a week — twenty. She put in her notice this morning. Got a job in the City at thirty-two. I said to her — '

'Valerie was not like that, I take it?'

'Valerie? Oh, Valerie Scott! No. A very dependable girl. With us for five years. Always punctual and cheerful. Never more than an hour for lunch.'

Bundy swivelled in his chair and pointed out of the window across the High Street. 'She always went to that little restaurant there for lunch at twelve, out by half past; then, if the weather was good, a bit of shopping or a stroll down by the river, and back by one.'

'What about going home in the evening? Did she always go off at the same time?'

'Half past four was her usual time, but if we were rushed she would always stay on. Not like some of them.'

'The day she died?'

'Half past four. I told the police that.'

He pointed out of the window again, 'That's the bus stop. She got the 441, up through Englefield Green then down through Old Windsor.'

'And there was nothing untoward that day — no unusual clients?'

'Nothing. She really had nothing to do with the clients. The police went into all that, believe me. They even questioned the clients. I lost some very profitable sales through it.'

'Tough!'

'It couldn't be helped,' said Bundy, bravely. 'Tragic! Tragic!'

Lynch got up. Where Inspector Gibb and Superintendent Matthews harvested, the gleaners starved; there was nothing here for him.

'You said you had been away for two years, did you not? If you were thinking of settling in this area we have one or two very attractive properties — '

For a moment Lynch toyed with the idea of telling him what he could do with his attractive properties, but he refrained from putting his improbable suggestions into words.

‘My plans are a little fluid, right now, but, if I think of settling down, I’ll bear you in mind, Mr Bundy, I’ll bear you in mind.’

Outside, he crossed, through the congealing traffic, to the exotically named ‘Roxanne’ and went inside to the clatter of teacups and the smell of freshly baked scones.

‘Just a pot of tea,’ he said to the elderly waitress who stood over him as he sat down.

Around him, elderly matrons rested their bones and their parcels and grumbled about the price of coffee and last night on the telly. The restaurant was small, and clean, and determinedly gay. On the glass topped table in front of him stood the luncheon menu: ‘Roast Lamb and Mint Sauce, Curried Beef, Bakewell Tart, Coffee Extra.’ It would have been exactly the same, vowed Lynch, the day Valerie Scott ate her last lunch there. Ordinary, English, unexciting, a world away from assassination.

Lynch filled his pipe, poured out the tea, and then looked at the case of Valerie

Scott. Only there wasn't any case. The trail was not just cold: it had never been. Gibb and Mathews were the best and they had got precisely nowhere. What chance for him! The army's maxim 'Never re-inforce failure' was a good one. It had to be. It had taken four years of the first World War and millions of dead good men to buy it.

The army! For no good reason he remembered a week in Toulon when he won £200 at poker, bought up the whisky ration of ten stranded padres and finished up on the blazing beach at Bandol with a wild wench, with coarse black hair and a mission of liberation. He felt a savage stab of need for the vivid colours and passions of the Mediterranean. He could get a plane to Nice that night —

'Your bill, sir.' The elderly waitress was tart, and frowning at his pipe, and a flushed dowager was eyeing his chair as if it were Shangri-La; her corns were giving her hell.

He paid and left.

The town clock struck half past four, and, at the bus stop by the cinema school-children were magnetised like iron filings. The car seat was hot enough to make him squirm as he drove back towards the bridge and braked to let a double-decker lumber round on to it. A 441. The timetable hadn't changed in two years.

Lynch followed a couple of car lengths behind, idling at the kerb while it disgorged and swallowed at the bus stops. Back again to the Egham roundabout, up the hill, then suddenly right, off the A 30, climbing more steeply. The Air Force Memorial sign in blue and white. Then the open heath where Valerie Scott was cut down, that very dependable girl.

The bus stopped and discharged a lone schoolgirl with swinging satchel. It drew away again, but he did not follow. He switched off, and from the pocket took up the crumpled file Price-Carruthers had given him, and Scott's letter, still unopened. From the file he tore out the sketch map, boldly drawn in black and red inks. He oriented it easily. Valerie Scott had alighted at the very bus stop where he now sat, and the narrow distinctive blaze the schoolgirl was taking across the grass was the same path an older girl had followed two years before.

To the right of the path, and nearly 250 yards from where he sat a little clump of trees and bush rose up like an island — the sniper's nest. A line of retreat to the thick copse behind it would be wholly masked. As Lynch watched the schoolgirl swung left with the path. Valerie Scott had been killed just before she reached the elbow. Not such a difficult shot from the hide, for you had the target face on. Let her turn at the elbow and you shortened the range but you had her in silhouette and reduced the chance of a killing shot. The marksman wanted her dead, not just shot.

He got out and walked to the sniper's nest. Trees and bushes. Nothing else. Twenty yards beyond it the sanctuary of the copse. He wound slowly through the close set trees and down to the unmade road beyond, to come silently on a small blue coupé parked on the verge. For a moment, the couple, locked in petrified embrace were unaware of him, then the man unglued his full red lips.

'Bloody peeping Tom!' he shouted.

Hurriedly, the girl buttoned her blouse, her head bowed, as Lynch skirted the car on to the road.

'You have a nice day for it,' he remarked sociably, as he started up the rise, 'as long as the rain keeps away.'

The rough gravel surface was wide enough for two cars, but was obviously little used — courting couples know where to go. Behind him, the blue car coughed into life, skidded into a tearing U-turn, and roared away in diminishing defiance. Some precious moments can never be recaptured.

Abruptly, the dirt road refined itself into tarmac, and, on his left the path from the bus stop tagged on, like a poor relation. Suddenly, there were small houses on either side, flaunting new paint, trimmed hedges, and postage stamp front lawns — Siamese twins in lipstick and party frocks.

He looked at the sketch map for a second, then went on. Fifty paces took him to Number 37 where Valerie Scott had lived with her father. Two down and three up, brave in yellow plaster and newly hung, wrought-iron gate. A pram shone below the front window and a great lilac decayed by the dividing fence.

The house stared blankly at him and said nothing.

He turned and went back by the path across the heath to his car,

For ten minutes he sat smoking and gazing at the tranquil tree fringed green. Nothing moved on it. A college bell tolled the death of learning. Another bus, ground up, slowed, then pulled away again without stopping. He opened Scott's letter.

'Dear Mr Lynch,

My daughter is dead. There was no need for anyone to kill her, but somebody did. I ask you to find the killer and see to the justice. If you cannot, you cannot. But the money is yours whether you succeed, or fail, or don't even try.

Yours faithfully,
Richard Scott

They never get the message thought Lynch sadly. Two thousand years of Knight Errants selling lily white maids to the fattest purse, of the dragon gobbling St George, daily and still the Scotts of the world imagined that wrongs were righted, good triumphed over evil in the end, and kind hearts were more than coronets. They had their rose-coloured spectacles issued at the baptismal font so that they could look at an ex-con and see a crusader. For his two thousand plus pounds Richard Scott should have had Don Quixote, the Marquis of Queensberry, and Roland of Roncevalles with all his lances. Instead, he got a disreputable Glasgow bully boy whose altruism was slightly less than vestigial. They couldn't win.

He started up the car, and let in the clutch very slowly. He was glad it was two thousand pounds and not two hundred.

4

It was nearly six by the time he reached Datchet. The traffic arteries were hardened with homebound traffic, and the level crossing gates were shut: he was sure that every time he came to Datchet they were shut. Commuters sat patiently in their cars, listening to their radios and devouring their evening papers. On his left, the molten river flowed so slowly as to seem still; a small boy sat on the grassy bank and idly dabbled his feet. On his right were biggish well cared for houses, flush with the pavement, hinting at old grandeurs with Victoria and Albert at Windsor.

Up ahead an engine started up.

As the cars rolled forward, he saw the house he was looking for, a tiny two storey miniature in black and white, wedged between Victorian masses. 'Salutations' the swinging wooden name plate announced.

He whipped his car across the oncoming traffic and fitted its length neatly into the run-in before 'Salutations' garage. How mock can one get, he wondered, a Tudor garage! Through the open door he saw a fawn Mini nestling cosily inside. The strip between house and pavement was laid with brightly coloured slabs in gay mosaic; green and yellow rain barrels, bellied like aldermen, stood on either side of the open front door. It was a trim well cared for little house, clean and starched like a cathedral choir boy.

Lynch stepped into a cool hall of white panelling, broken by blue doors on each side; at the far end another blue door stood ajar, framing a segment of blue sky, leafy branches, and massed roses.

'Anybody home?' he called.

'Through here,' carolled a girl's voice.

The garden was no wider than the frontage, long and narrow; trees and flowering shrubs hung in tapestry against the high enclosing walls. The grass was crew cut, lush with much watering. At the far end a girl sat on a candy striped reclining chair, with her back to him. Her white shorts and halter were vivid paint slashes on a body tanned so deep that there was a brown shimmer as she moved. She was vigorously drying her shining black hair in a foam of red towel.

'I'll be with you in a moment. I can't stand wet hair.'

'No hurry,' said Lynch, 'every prospect pleases — '

' — And only man is vile. I was only going to sunbathe, but the river looked so tempting.'

'I blamed the level crossing for the traffic jam.'

She stood up, laughing, and turned to face him, as she dropped the towel on the grass and shook herself.

Thank God for honesty, thought Lynch; most women would have draped the towel over themselves in moist mock modesty. She was tall, for a girl; black hair cascaded silkily over wide, shapely shoulders to large firm breasts; long legs tapered from wide hips. How could she be so big and so slender at the same time? Perhaps her face was overlong for conventional prettiness, the jaw line boldly etched. A stupid chit would have plucked thin the pronounced black eyebrows and would have detracted from the dancing blue eyes. Not beautiful, but vivid and pleasing to see, and feminine, and passionate, too, for the right man. Whoever he was, Lynch envied him.

'What can I do for you, sir?'

'Talk, just talk.'

'I like that. Why don't you sit down.'

He put the case down between them, and stretched out on his stomach on the warm grass; she went back to the striped canvas.

'It's been a bitty sort of day — until now. You MUST be Frances Gavin.'

She nodded.

'I apologise for the image I had. My lady teachers were either fat, smelly porkers or dessicated porkers; every man jack of them. Education has made great strides. My name is Lynch.'

'Mr Scott's detective! I hoped you'd come. Nobody thought you would do anything.'

'Nobody?'

'The lawyer, you know, plushbottom;

the police. The general view was that you would take the money and scarper.'

'Not your view?'

She grinned, 'I don't have to apologise for my image of you.'

'Another dewy-eyed romantic! But thank you just the same.'

'What's that? Your Private Eye Outfit?'

Lynch pulled the case towards him and flipped open the catches.

'Tape recorder — portable — battery driven — for you to talk into.'

'About Valerie? I've said it all — over and over; to her father, to the police.'

She caught her breath, 'And to myself. How many times to myself!'

He took time over his pipe.

'That's it; the case couldn't be deader. Every lead that could be followed, the police followed. You could wager your dowry on that.'

'I need a dowry you think?'

'As of this moment I am prepared to offer your father fourteen milch cows, two bullocks, and my second best hunting spear. You need only bring the cooking pots.'

'My father will consult the elders. Meanwhile let's get back to this tape recorder thing.'

'Right. You talk about Valerie. Anything, everything. Whatever you remember, as far back as you can go. The machine drinks it all in and I play it back, and maybe, it's an enormous maybe, somewhere in what you say, there's a pointer. Absolutely original method — nine out of ten fictional detectives use it. Are you a betting woman?'

'Only over the sticks, I hibernate in the flat season.'

'The odds are enormous that you can resurrect anything that might give us a clue — astronomical, but, as I see it, there isn't anything else for me to try.'

'It could be a long job and nothing to show at the end of it.'

'That is the near certainty. But if the genesis of Valerie's murder lies in her ordinary everyday life, then you may be the only key. On the other hand, she might have been killed by accident, by mistake, or by a madman.'

'I see. And if you get nothing from me?'

'I fulfill everyone's expectations and get the first plane to Nice.'

'I wouldn't like that. I'll do my best. Would you like a beer?'

'Consider yourself elected Girl of the Year. I thought you only lived in the better books.'

He got up and threw his linen jacket down on the grass, 'I'll find it without a hazel twig.'

The kitchen was white and compact, with red tiles on the floor. The draining board held a pile of exercise books and a volume entitled 'Introduction to Calculus'. Lynch shuddered and sought the refrigerator. He filled two pewter tankards with Lager and as many ice cubes as the beer would allow, and bore them like an altar server, back into the garden.

'To first meetings!' toasted Frances and buried her face in froth.

'And to kindly girls who keep pewter tankards in the kitchen.'

'Daddy's,' she explained, 'he and mother live, more or less, permanently in New York. He's an accountant, but nice.'

She took a large swig and Lynch watched the play of muscles in her brown throat. 'He introduced me to beer very young.'

'An enlightened parent; I will throw in my very best hunting spear and ten goats.'

She giggled and beer ran down her chin. Lynch switched on the tape recorder.

'When did you first meet her?'

'At school: the same one I teach at now. I was eleven. I was a week late in starting because of German measles, and all the other girls knew their way around and were very superior and patronising. All except Valerie; she showed me the lavs, and the cubby holes where the big girls smoked, and the broken shower that scalded you. Important thing to an eleven year old.'

'How come you and she went to the same school?'

'You mean we had money and they didn't?'

There was nothing indirect about this lass thought Lynch. He nodded.

'We didn't always have it. Valerie was

an only child, like me, and both of us had good parents who grudged us nothing. Maybe that's why we got on so well, being only children. Oh, I don't know. Why bother to analyse it? We just liked each other. Wait a minute.'

She rose in an undulation of long dusky legs and disappeared into the house. Lynch drank his cold beer slowly and gazed at the roses with affection, there hadn't been any roses in Govan.

'Some snaps of Val and me.'

She flopped down beside him, damp and sweet smelling, throwing back her black shining hair with a fluid impatient gesture.

'There are masses of others, but these were handy and they're fairly recent.'

He stared long at a fair, smiling girl eating an ice cream on a sunwashed beach. A rosy serene girl. He could see why Frances had liked her. Given the chance he would have liked her too. The second snap showed her in a dirndl skirt and a gypsy blouse, with a bicycle as a prop.

'Three years ago — we cycled over to

Maidenhead one Sunday afternoon, and had tea at Skindles. I had the camera with me. That one came out rather well.'

'You do a lot of cycling?'

'I used to, with Val; not now.'

He turned over the last snapshot.

'That was the last one that was taken of her, about three months before she was killed; it was a very pricey ball at Windsor.'

Four of them were imprisoned for ever in the photographer's flashlight; Valerie, wide-eyed in ballet length foam of white tulle: Frances, sheathed in black velvet, a champagne glass raised to her lips, two personable young men in dinner jackets and cummerbunds.

'What about the man?'

'Derek? He was in Kenya when she was killed, still is.'

'What about the other one, scorching your cleavage with his hot little eyes?'

'Jimmy? Oh, he's sweet.'

'Yours?'

'Oh no! He's his mummy's. I'm not one for cutting umbilical cords.'

He put the gypsy girl carefully into his

wallet, 'I'll keep this one for a bit: it's well defined.'

'I'll want it back, eventually.'

They were silent for a long five minutes, comfortably, without strain.

'You never make friends like the ones you grow up with,' she said. 'Over the years the wrinkles are ironed out, the fences taken down, you've shared tears and rivalries and disappointments. You're in each others' lives. You live your own and hers as well. It's warm and easy and part of you.'

'You have to leave them in the end.'

'Maybe. But that's slower, part of growing older. It's not — ' she shuddered, 'like an amputation. I miss her.'

'How often did you see each other?'

'We were in and out of each other's houses. She did the Latin and the History; I was hot on the Maths and the Sciences. When we had done our homework, there would be coffee and toast, and we'd listen to records, or spin our technicolor futures together, and giggle. Even homework was fun.'

And so it could be, thought Lynch, and

he had a sour look back to a boy hunched over Virgil in the one room that was home. Over head the damp washing dripped maddeningly on his neck; his mother ironed on the other two thirds of the one table; his father spat with a splutter into the hot grate; and, outside in the street, frenzied ululations betokened freer and wiser boys at football. Thus was a great classical scholar lost to the world.

Or was he? What about wee John Downie upstairs in replicated surroundings, his daemon surviving rickets and war, and well fed competition to put him in the Chair of Humanities? Pat Lynch, thou shalt not kid thyself!

Frances called him back from the muddled Forties.

'That was the year we went youth hostelling in Italy and met the mad Americans in Venice — real ones, who didn't have a ranch, or a couple of oil wells in the back garden. Actually, they were pretty broke; and we were nearly arrested for singing 'Old Man River' in a gondola.'

Outside, cars coughed into life as the level crossing gates opened once again. He went back into the kitchen and refilled the tankards, and brought them back into the garden; then he lay beside her, drinking his beer, and smoking; and watched her, sprawled on her stomach, lifting her leg, lazily, over her trim bottom. And she talked on, flicking over the album of their lives. Ordered, happy lives till someone put a bullet in them. Sometimes you could do this for people, open the floodgates of their lives and let memory pour out in great swirling torrents. Sometimes. Not often.

'She really liked old Bundy at the office. You've met him, have you? He's pompous and full of himself but decent, basically. None of this paternal hand on your waist lark, and telling you what a lovely figure you have, and then 'Presto!', before you know where you are that same paternal hand is away on a voyage of exploration.'

Lynch grinned, 'I always found that a pretty successful approach, but I thought it was original.'

'Men! It was corny in the Garden of Eden!' She turned her sparkling blue eyes on him. 'Anyway, the approach doesn't matter: if a woman likes you it makes no difference whether you recite the Department of Trade's weekly returns, whatever they are, or the Song of Solomon. Where was I? Oh, yes! I was the one with the great unrealisable ambitions. I was going to be Eve Curie, or Virginia Woolf, or the first Lady Chancellor. All Val ever wanted was a good husband, four children, and a seaside house. She was quite, quite firm about the seaside house: it had to be in Somerset. Don't ask me why. I don't know: neither did she.'

Outside, silence had smoothed the road down, and tired breadwinners were taking their full bellies into their gardens or their locals.

'You say she went to church on Sundays. Unusual these days. Which denomination?'

'Anglican like me. We went through the traditional reaction against church and State in our teens, of course, but we got over it. We helped with the Darby and

Joan Club, and we attended Morning Service, and Evensong; we liked Evensong best. Which denomination are you? Or are you any? I mean I shouldn't expect that in your business — ' she faltered.

'I'm a lapsed Mick,' said Lynch, softly, 'but still a Mick, I suppose, grow up a Mick in a Calvinist country and it bites deep. But go on about Valerie.'

She went on, and time slipped gently through their hands as the shadows inched over the lawn. Lynch relaxed listening.

A hand shook him.

'York ham and potato salad, fresh strawberries and Devon cream.'

He rubbed his eyes and sat up, 'And some more cool beer.'

'English cheese and freshly ground coffee, and if you help with the washing up, some Drambuie out of Dad's bottle, but not too much because it's the only thing he's possessive about.'

He got to his feet and she stretched a hand for him to pull her up. Ruefully, he noted that with high heels she'd probably be an inch or two taller than he. 'That's quite a knack you have there, Frances, reading what my mind is going to think before it actually gets round to thinking it. The E.S.P. lads would love you. Do you mind if I call you Frances?'

'If I did I should have objected an hour ago. What do I call you?'

'Pat. And I didn't notice. But I must have known you for a hundred years at least.' She laughed easily, and, unthinking, he flung his arm round her bare, warm shoulder, as they walked towards the house.

She jerked a thumb behind them at the tape recorder, 'What about Big Brother?'

'Let him find his own girl,' said Lynch, but he went back for it just the same.

They ate in the narrow dining room with the french windows open to the fragrance of the garden. Lynch had found some Shearing and Garner records, and they left the doors open so that the music crept in on them, muted and a little melancholy, from the sitting room.

By the time the washing up was done the shadows had coalesced and engulfed the lawn, and the moon was striking silver on the river.

He moved the tape recorder into the sitting room, and they had their coffee and Drambuie, and still Frances talked on. He rinsed the cups and glasses, without interrupting her, and then sat down and refilled his pipe until eventually she fell silent.

'You're talked out. Let's take a walk and look at the water and not say a word.'

She nodded. He switched off the tape recorder and took her arm, and together they strolled out into the warm Summer dark.

They went by dim woods and quiet lanes, following the silver swathe of the water, then leaving it for a grassy ride, which skirted the houses and flung an arm round a slight shadowed rise. The distant susuration of tyres was a grace note in the melodious quiet. It was a time, thought Lynch, for lovers' promises and old men's memories, and he wondered, wryly, where he fitted. Then he forgot to wonder and held the warm supple arm in his a little more tightly, and let himself be led contentedly over the extravagant, moonlit landscape.

An hour later they stood once more in the open doorway of 'Salutations'.

'Some things have a perfection you can only know and never describe. Frances. Thank you.'

He made to put on the hall light but her hand stayed him: he stood where he was, unmoving. Her arms came round his shoulders and she kissed him lovingly, lingeringly.

'I wanted to kiss you and I have, and I want you to make love to me but you're not going to.'

He put his fingers on the smoothness of her cheek.

'There would be a good reason?'

'Yes, there would be. I think, perhaps I have too much love in me to give it to the first starving man to cross my threshold. That's about the only way I can put it.'

'There's not an honest argument I could use against that, though maybe there are one or two slightly bent ones I could try, but my heart wouldn't be in them.'

She moved his hand down to her full breast and held it there with her own, then she moved away and switched on the light. They looked at one another blinking. 'Wise lady. Whoever gets you will want no other — ever.'

She disappeared into the sitting room and returned with the tape recorder.

'Home, Pat Lynch. Back to your gilded garret.'

Together they went to his car, and he put the tape recorder in the back.

'To quote a doughtier warrior than myself 'I shall return'.'

'You'd better, or I'll hunt you down.'

Quickly her lips brushed his cheek.

He drove back to the 'Crusader' and it was only when he was drifting into sleep that he realised that he could not recall one yard of the journey, not one bend, not one gear change. He opened his eyes to the dark. Damn it! He couldn't even remember putting the light out.

5

'Come on, Lynch, skilly's up!'

He opened his eyes to a glacier of pink candy floss moving inexorably towards the bed — Biddy in a satin marquee, bearing a pintsized mug of tea.

'A rose red city — '

'Half as old as time!' she finished and tilted the mug over his navel, perilously. 'You can have it amidships, you undersized Glasgow keelie, or you can be nice.'

'Decisions yet, at sparrowfart.' He grabbed the mug and scalded his lips. 'Biddy, I love you, and if I can get my old platoon together we'll marry you.'

Biddy grinned, 'You'd see more action than you ever saw in any bloody battlefield, I promise you that.'

She moved over to the window and leaned out, 'Blue sky and sun; it's going to be another spanking day. I don't know what the hell this country's coming to. Not one decent cold wet English

Summer's day for months. The tourists are feeling cheated. What are you doing today, Lynch? In? Out?'

'In till after lunch, anyway. I am going to lie among the peacocks and do a little work.'

By tradition, breakfast at the 'Crusader' was English country house, but so muffled as to be a mime. A solitary waiter stood at the long sideboard to replenish the silver covered serving dishes in a whisper. Lynch swore they put silencers on the teapots. He helped himself to kidneys, bacon, sausages, toast, and a pot of tea. Then he found himself a table by the great french windows. Four unopened morning papers rested on each table. He turned over the 'Times' and tried to do the crossword in his head. He was always trying to do it in his head, which was odd, because he couldn't do it the ordinary way. By the time he had finished breakfast he had found three answers which was par for the course.

'Thus proving,' he said to himself, 'that I still occupy the intellectual low ground that I did two years ago.'

He got himself an exercise book and pencil from Charles, and took the tape recorder to a secluded spot in the garden. The first playback took him to eleven o'clock and a still empty exercise book. He found the place where he had dozed off in Frances Gavin's garden and played it again.

Valerie's stand on pre-marital sex — she was against it. Good for her! As for Frances. Hm!

The first time they drove on the M1 to see Coventry Cathedral and how they had to stick to the slow lane because Valerie had this thing about fast driving. And how she had dozed off on the way back and Frances had let the Mini out.

The fiasco of the Ladies' Doubles at the tennis club.

What was there to adumbrate violence and sudden death from a single rifle shot on an empty heath?

Nothing!

He switched off and took himself back in for coffee. The first wave of Jags. and Mercs. had washed up against the steps for pre-lunch drinkies. He found Biddy sitting on the table in the stone flagged kitchen swinging her great graceful legs, and drinking coffee out of a ten gallon beaker.

'I've just poured yours,' she said. 'I didn't think you'd have the strength.'

They talked happily about nothing at all, and then he made his way back to his bosky den, rewound the tape, and started all over again.

The morning wore on, the heat thickened and oozed relentlessly through his cellular shirt; the 'Crusader' shimmered in the haze.

By lunch time he had played three quarters of the tape through again and his notebook was still empty. He switched it off and opened the file Price-Carruthers had given him, leafing through the newspaper cuttings. The national dailies had played the murder big for a couple of days — good pictures, with white dots and arrows depicting the flight of the bullet, and the probable path of the murderer. One of them had photographed from a helicopter. For the local papers it had been manna from Heaven:

two of the weeklies had kept it front page for four weeks.

He wondered whether Price-Carruthers had noticed the irony of an advertisement by Trott, Chudleigh appearing in a corner of the page which carried the inquest on Trott, Chudleigh's typist. Was that what the Sunday Supplements had called 'network' a few years before?

On the back of another cutting he read:

'Crime Began By Accident.'

'In sentencing James Maidment, garage storekeeper, to three months' imprisonment for embezzlement, the magistrate observed that but for the accident of a customer walking off without a receipt, Maidment might never have embarked on the course which brought him into the dock . . . '

Was that it? Did Valerie Scott's death reach back in time to some trivial accident like the luckless storekeeper's?

He gathered up the recorder, the file, and the empty exercise book, and wended his way back to a peerless lunch.

Afterwards, he lay on the grass, hands canonical on a drum-tight stomach, drowsily triangulating the landscape of liquidation.

Family mayhem? With only a doting father?

Crime passionel? And Frances Gavin insensitive to the passion? Hardly.

Murder by mistake? And never rectified?

Murder for profit? Yes, but whose?

Murder for fun. One frolic in two years? Unlikely, but keep it in the pending file.

Whichever contour you followed, the size tens had already trodden, measured, careful. The trig point had to be the marksman. Find him and you got your bearings. But the law men hadn't been able to. And they had all the resources. Or had they? There was one they didn't have. Lynch didn't have it, either; but he had an I O U he could call in.

He went indoors.

The voice at the other end of the line was terse and hostile.

Lynch sighed.

‘If he won’t be back till tomorrow afternoon then he won’t. No. Just say an old friend from boarding school.’

He hung up.

When a hiatus like this happened, he always started thinking about fishing — and wishing he liked it. He didn’t. So, usually, he ended up in the Victoria and Albert, looking at carpets. That he did like. Besides, he hadn’t been there for at least a couple of years.

6

He presented himself twenty-four hours later.

In Soho space must earn, so the tiny office sported only a small-boned desk, a settee, and a laden drinks trolley. The man, open armed on the threshold, was a rangy cockney ram-rod with thinning sandy hair, and a wide grin unexpectedly jewelled with three gold teeth. Legend reported them the trophy of an old bullion robbery, spectacular and unsolved. Cappy always smiled hugely at the men from the Met.

'Pat, old son! They sprung you at last then?'

'Didn't want to, Cappy, but they needed the cell for an unfrocked bishop.' The other pumped his hand, pushed him down on the settee and poured two half tumblersful from a dusty bottle which he deposited, uncorked by Lynch's right foot.

'Here's to freedom, Pat. Nothing like the nick to make you appreciate it, eh? You know the first thing I always do when they let me out? Stick my tongue out! I can taste it, Pat. No kidding! I can flaming taste it.'

Lynch savoured the twelve year old elixir and looked fondly at his host. Cappy Carpenter. Not a king. There were no kings any longer in the underworld. But a prince in his own fiefdom of clubs, pubs, massage parlours, betting shops, minicabs. A freebooter who, in palmier days would have been out with Drake and Morgan but was making the best of his own times.

'If this is social, Pat, I've got a bird in the show downstairs who's just your style. I'll give her a buzz and we'll — '

'Not today, Cappy, thanks. Haven't got my strength back yet. But I do need a favour.'

'Anything, Pat. You know that. I owe you.'

Occasionally, the condottiere has to show the enemy, and his own troops, that he still has bottle. So, instead of sending in the mercenaries, Cappy had put the frighteners on an upstart rival, personally. He had bargained for the six months he had drawn, but not for the crazed old lag who would have threaded a sharpened saucepan handle through his right kidney but for Lynch's outstretched foot.

'I need to talk to Willy Pascoe.'

'Jesus, Pat! You know you can have anything I've got, but I haven't got Willy Pascoe; nobody has. Look, you've done bird and all that, but you're still a punter, you're not one of us. You tell me why and I'll try, Pat, I'll really try; but by God it won't be easy.'

It wasn't. But half an hour and two long phone calls later they were both standing outside a newsagent's in the congeries of lanes and passages west of Tottenham Court Road. The shop window was opaque with a patchwork quilting of postcards and sun curled flimsies which Lynch was just able to sample and no more as Cappy fumbled for the latch.

'Inge, Swedish Therapist.'

'Mademoiselle Suzanne, French Lessons.'

'Carrie Kane, Craftswoman in Leather.'

'The lifeblood of commerce,' he murmured to Cappy.

'Accommodation addresses, too, if you ever need one,' the other replied as they went in.

An amiable man like an elderly grocer reigned over a gallery of mammary potraiture and a library of goatish primers.

He raised his eyes from his Midday Standard, 'Cappy.'

'Jack. Willy's expecting us.'

Jack waved his reeking Gaulois at a glass panelled door at the rear and returned to the starting prices.

The back shop was an Edwardian kitchen, with, despite the summer warmth, a low fire burning in the grate, and a black iron kettle hissing contentedly on the hob. Behind a rectangular table, covered with a green chenille cloth sat Willy Pascoe, sipping coffee from a half pint mug, a glowing cheroot in his left hand.

He motioned them to the scrubbed white chairs on the other side of the table, facing him, and Lynch seated himself on Cappy's right.

The man opposite was a dainty dumpling with a smooth, rosy face, thatched with well tended, white hair. Seventy, seventy-five, a left over from vanished music hall, 'female impersonator' not 'drag artist' and nothing gay or off-beat about this diminutive relic.

'He's not in the trade, Cappy.' The voice was strong, projected.

'I'll guarantee him, though.'

The unfaded baby blue eyes engaged Lynch, 'You nobbled Strapper, got two years. Before that, an office in Clarges Street, wasn't it?'

Lynch nodded. The encyclopaedist wasn't showing off, just functioning.

In the world of top flight bandsmen when you wanted to mount an orchestra you called a number in the Charing Cross Road to find out who was available. In the world of serious crime when you wanted to empty a bank vault you called on Willy Pascoe. He knew which thermal lancer was being pressed for alimony, where the best wheelman was 'curled up tight'. Unlike Scotland Yard, all his archives were kept in his head.

'What do you want?'

The ageing cherub heard him out without interrupting, only refilling his beaker from an earthenware jug, and kindling a fresh cheroot.

'A rifleman to rent,' he mused, when Lynch was done, 'or a psycho killing for glee. Perhaps one and the same: business and pleasure together? Two years ago?' He shook his head, 'Rifle's a bit outré for the trade; shotgun, pistol, shiv, piano wire; you can hire those, but a rifle! No! Too remote, too chancy. Amateurish. Wait, though! That Fusilier, Cappy, that was two years ago.'

'The deserter from Ulster? Took off with an armoury; a nutter! Hawked himself around Kilburn for a while, but no takers, not even the Provos.'

'None,' affirmed Willy, 'but he was around that Summer — May, June. Fusilier Lockett, came from a village in Cambridgeshire.'

'Anyway I can get in touch with?'

They shook their heads simultaneously.

'Went out of business about the end of June,' explained Cappy. 'Nutters are bad for all of us.'

Lynch didn't press; the Trade followed the Biblical Union Rule: 'If an eye offend thee, pluck it out.'

'There doesn't seem to have been a similar kind of murder since,' Lynch pointed out. 'It could have been him — for fun or for fee.'

'Possible,' admitted Willy, 'but unlikely. If Lockett was hired I ought to have heard. Still. One more thing. Harsbroke the village was, if that's any use to you.'

The audience was over. They stood up and Cappy felt for his wallet; it would be a breach of protocol for Lynch to offer.

'Token, Cappy.' Willie held up five fingers, 'Strapper bilked me — once.'

The crisp five vanished into the little man's top pocket; he inclined his head, regally, 'Cappy. Mr Lynch.'

The Head dismissing two prefects.

Outside, Cappy was dogmatic, 'You're not going to find Lockett, Pat. My word on it. Better to come with me and rehabilitate yourself with a few jars.'

'I know I'm not going to find him, but if he did it, and if he did it for wages I might just get a line on his master.'

'You won't. Nobody pays your stamp on a job like that. But you'll go your own way; I know you.'

'We'll have the jars, Cappy, and soon. I promise.'

They made their farewells and Cappy strode off, cock of his own walk, the squire's gold teeth flashing at the tenantry.

Lynch reclaimed his car and made his way Northwards. He got a clear passage through Camden Town and Upper Holloway on to the A1 and settled down to the sixty mile run, pushing hard.

Harsbroke didn't appear on his maps, but a friendly bus driver in Royston placed it just off the A10 leading to Cambridge.

'It's easy to miss the turning,' he cautioned.

It was. He passed it twice but didn't mind too much. Cambridgeshire was worth rediscovering, flat, grave, and fertile, its ancient granges and hamlets digesting the twentieth century without haste. Still Angle land, moated from the outside world by the Great North Road.

Harsbroke, when he came to it, was a by-passed tithing of thatch and white-wash, huddled for security round the sturdy keep of its Norman church.

The potman was reserved, but courteous.

'Granny Lockett that would be. The second house up Vicarage Lane.'

Lynch took the tankard over to an empty table, scarred like a butcher's block. Around him the half dozen locals sat watchful, linked in silence against the outlander. Not a domino moved. Harsbroke wasn't on the tourist circuit.

He drank the ale quickly and left, the door, swinging behind him and wafting the growl of re-started colloquy.

Crabtree Cottage was a low-roofed cot, hunkered behind a green-pricked vegetable plot, nursed and fecund. The door swung open at his first knock, as if Granny Lockett had been telepathically alerted from the tap room.

She was in her eighties, lean and spry,

with beady black eyes, and thinning white hair, taut to a coiled bun. At her throat a cameo brooch gathered the high collar of her shiny floral dress.

'I'm not from the army or the police,' he explained patiently, for the second time, 'if I can find out what he's been doing since he left the army, it may help me in another matter.'

'Deserted,' she corrected. It was in her mind to slam the door in his face, he could see, but she relented, finally, and ushered him into a small neat parlour, dominated by a tall, carved harmonium. She didn't invite him to sit.

'Easter Saturday, 1975,' she recounted in a flat, unemotional voice, 'the Vicar came down with a policeman from Cambridge. Deserted they said. He's never come here, never will; nor as I'd want him. My son's boy; he died and she left so I brought him up as I could. But he was wild, like her. It's quiet here; we don't take to wildness.'

'And you haven't heard from him?'

'No, mister, not since he went for a soldier.'

'And nobody's been here asking for him, or written to him?'

'Vicar asked me once. That's all.'

'Is there anyone else he might have got in touch with?'

'Didn't have no friends.'

There was certainty in the shrewd, unyielding face that had to be accepted. He wondered how she would react if he told her she would never see her grandson again, but decided that she knew that already on some deep, instinctive level.

He bade her goodnight and let himself out into the deserted lane. Behind him the Church bell chimed sonorously, raising a company of excited, chattering starlings. Seven o'clock. If he hurried he would have time for a walk round the Backs and a latish dinner in Cambridge. His journey would not have been totally wasted.

7

Next morning, after breakfast, he strolled down Petty Curie and bought some tobacco, before paying his hotel bill and collecting his car from the hotel garage.

The journey back was low paced and thoughtful, but no blinding flash encompassed him. The Lynch locker was shotless.

At Kew he stopped for sandwiches and beer and toyed with the notion of going to Staines and browsing through the back numbers of one of the local papers. It wasn't the most brilliant idea he had ever hatched, nobody was going to leap out of the bath with it; in fact it wasn't an idea at all, only a way of passing the afternoon, but it was all he could come up with. He drove on to Staines.

The Staines Banner slumbered in a cluster of small sheds and brick buildings which a psuedo Roman front failed to make impressive.

'Archives?' sneered the man in Reception, 'Where do you think you are? Printing House Square! Forty years ago this was a jobbing printers.'

He was middle aged and rumpled, with a brandy drinker's face, and shrewd eyes. 'In fact, you're standing in the original shop now.'

'Are you in charge, chum? Or do they just keep you here to give the guided tour and tell the folksy stories?'

The man grinned.

'I am the editor-in-chief, reporter-in-chief and in-singular, and the pauper proprietor. My name is Crisp. I am also surrogate for the old hen who usually answers bloody silly questions: she's in the loo. What do you want the archives for?'

'I'm getting up an anthology of Prose Gems from the Provincial Papers. I thought of putting you between James Agate and Emile Zola.'

'And up yours!' said Crisp amiably, 'Come on, I'll show you the back numbers.'

He led the way up a tenuous wooden staircase.

'We keep them in the attics. The cellars are so damp we rent them out for regattas.'

The two connecting attic rooms were an agreeable surprise — well lit, well ventilated, and floored with coconut matting. There were two tables, writing pads, sharpened pencils.

Crisp flung a hand at deep shelves carrying giant brown volumes, 'Each volume holds a year's editions, work from left to right.'

The spine of each volume bore, in bold gilt lettering, the year; the left hand one was stamped '1946'.

'Whatever you want I can find it much quicker than you. I know these volumes like this month's bank statement.'

Crisp's inquisitiveness was unabashed; Lynch thought he must be a very good newspaperman.

'I don't know till I find it,' said Lynch. 'If I find it.'

'Forthcoming, aren't we! I could starve to death listening to blokes like you.

Come on, you're getting the quid, what about a little pro quo in my direction, eh?'

'It's a kind of geriatic study,' improvised Lynch, wildly, 'a regional analysis of longevity. If your 'Congratulations on Hundredth Birthday' stories are higher than the national average over the last ten years we do a study in depth of the area. Naturally, we send you a copy of our findings.'

Somewhere, under their feet there was a thumping of Bofors guns and the rush of a tidal wave.

'There's a geriatric study for you,' snarled Crisp when the cataclysm had subsided to mere thunder. 'Our plumbing! Somebody'll pull that chain too often and 'Boom'! The whole place will collapse about us.'

Lynch nodded sympathetically.

'Nobody will disturb you,' promised Crisp, opening the door. 'I'm the only one who uses it, 'Twenty Five Years Ago This Week', stuff like that. I'm off to the Townswomen's Guild.'

He closed the door only to re-open it a

second later. 'That geriatric lark's a load of old compost, but five out of ten for effort. And lay off our loo: we don't carry any third party insurance.'

He closed the door again.

Lynch started with the 1975 volume, found the first report of the Valerie Scott killing, and began to work back. Fetes, flower shows, court proceedings, shoplifting, indecent exposure, a flare up in the Council Chamber, a Peeping Tom, car crashes. The human comedy replayed weekly with crude and predictable variation. If this were the only legacy to some space traveller, prowling amid the radio-active dust, what a fractious, perverted lot we'd seem. But then only frailty was worth recording: bad news was the best news. He lifted out the 1974 volumes.

At four o'clock a middle aged sensible body in knitted twin set brought a mug of tea and a Danish pastry.

'He'll have nothing else,' she muttered cryptically, and vanished.

By the 1963 volume it was after five and he had achieved nothing but eyestrain and a growing sense of futility. He pushed the heavy book away and took out his tobacco pouch. Probably he was reaching too far back, anyway. Violence was seldom a slow burner.

Wearily, he hefted down the 1975 volume again. One more scan and then a dash to the nearest pub. It opened at December — must have been a merry Christmas for Richard Scott that year. He flipped over the pages a month at a time — October — September — August — July. He turned back again to August and the thick black headline that had flared at him momentarily:

WINDOW CLEANERS 'POLISH OFF' BUILDERS' HOLIDAY MONEY. DARING PAY-ROLL SNATCH AT STAINES. £90,000 MISSING.

Crisp was obviously Caption-Writer-in-Ordinary as well as everything else.

He read the text:

'Yesterday morning, at eleven, as shoppers walked unconcernedly past the Pritchard Building in the High Street, a drama straight out of the pages of fiction was being enacted, unsuspected, above their heads. Two thieves, posing as window-cleaners, entered the cashier's office of Brace & Clelland, the well known local building firm, where wages were being made up for hundreds of men on sites throughout the Home Counties. One man held the cashier, Mr Frederick Davies, and his two assistants at gun point; the second man forced all three to lie on the floor and submit to being bound and gagged.

At half-past eleven, police broke down the locked door at the request of the Office manager and found the helpless victims still on the floor. There was no sign of the 'window cleaners'. Some £90,000 is thought to be missing.

Police are anxious to trace a green Minivan with the sign 'Kleenglass Window Cleaners' painted in black letters on the side and on the back doors. The registration number is LYE 281D. Anyone who saw this vehicle yesterday should get in touch with the police.'

Lynch looked at the date of the issue:

Friday, 29th August, 1975 — the eve of the Summer Bank Holiday week-end, a lot of extra-full pay packets. An ideal time to lift them. Crisp must have had a hell of a rush redrafting his front page late on Thursday to get the story on the doorstep on Friday morning.

Interested, despite his aching eyeballs, he turned over to the following week's edition, the issue of the 5th September.

Crisp had used his week well — a photograph of the façade of the Pritchard Building, one of an internal courtyard, showing an extending ladder against a third storey window, an interior shot of the cashier's office, with Frederick Davies and his two assistants, unbound now. He obviously didn't give a fig for judicial restraint, or the laws of libel, because he had pulled out all the stops on the story.

COMMANDO CRIME

'Meticulous planning, patience, and audacious execution marked last Thursday's payroll grab at Brace & Clelland's,

Staines Building Giant. No spur-of-the-moment handbag snatch this. Contrariwise, as your reporters' timetable shows, the thieves' first steps to riches were taken A YEAR AGO. Painstakingly, Banner staff have joined piece to piece to reveal a crime fashioned with such foresight and daring as to rank among the brilliant coups of present day banditry.

12th June 1974: A man, giving the name of John Cooper, pays to Proffetts, Estate Agents, Ashford, £800, six months rent in advance for the lease of a furnished ground floor maisonette, at 4 Dennistoun Close, Ashford. Signs an 18 months agreement. References were taken up. When these were hastily re-checked this week, the addresses were found to be accommodation addresses. Probability is that Cooper, or accomplice, wrote the references.

17th June 1974: A man, giving the name John Cooper, and his address as 4 Dennistoun Close, Ashford, applies for work as a window cleaner with Kleenglass Window Cleaners, Kingston-upon-Thames. This small firm has, or had, the contract for the Pritchard Building in Staines. Window Cleaners have a very fast staff turnover, and Cooper was employed immediately. Claimed to have no National Insurance Card or tax papers because he had been working with a relative in Eire for many years.

September, 1974: Cooper is put on contract work with Thomas Grant a fellow employee at Kleenglass. They clean Brace & Clelland's windows every second Wednesday.

February, 1975: THURSDAY has become the day for Brace & Clelland's windows. 'No reason' say Kleenglass 'it just seemed to happen. We thought nothing of it at the time.'

Thursday, 28th August 1975 — D. Day

8.00 a.m.: Cooper and Grant leave Kleenglass, Kingston-upon-Thames — destination, Brace & Clellands, Staines

8.30 a.m.: Cooper and Grant arrive at 4 Dennistoun Close, Ashford, to make up Cooper's lunch time sandwiches. According to Grant, Cooper stated that he had overslept because his landlady(!) was away. Cooper makes a pot of tea as he 'had no breakfast'. Grant takes a cup, 'feels funny', falls asleep.

10.30 a.m.: Security men deliver £90,000 to cashier's office of Brace & Clelland.

10.35 a.m.: Cashier's office is locked from inside by cashier Davies.

10.40 a.m.: Kleenglass van drives into inner courtyard of Pritchard Building. Two men get out and erect ladder against third storey window. Witnessed by filing clerk of Valley Toy Company who thereafter 'paid no attention'.

10.55 a.m.: Two masked men enter cashier's office through connecting door to cashier's lavatory. One carries pistol, the other a shotgun. One of them, 'with a kind of North Country accent' orders staff to lie down on floor; the other, who did not speak, ties their hands and feet with twine and put broad bands of medical tape over their mouths.

11.25 a.m.: Police break into cashier's office. £90,000 missing. No sign of masked men.

12.30 p.m.: Police raid 4 Dennistoun Close, Ashford: find Thomas Grant unconscious, but otherwise unharmed.

Friday, 29th August: Attendant at Staines Bridge car park finds Kleenglass Minivan LYE 281D abandoned in car park. 'Probably there all night.'

Tuesday, 2nd September: Police issue the following description of the man known as John Cooper whom they wish to interview in connection with their enquiries. '5 feet 8 inches in height, stockily built, ruddy complexion, collar length black hair with thick sideboards and handle bar moustache, wears dark tinted spectacles. When last seen was dressed in blue overalls and grey cloth cap.'

The accompanying police artist's impression was mainly facial hairiness and overlarge dark glasses.

Take away the hair and the glasses and who have you got? Lynch asked himself. Anybody. Nobody.

Quickly he thumbed through editions between September, 1975 and May, 1977, but there was nothing, not a whisper of wages or window cleaners. Even allowing for Crisp's highly coloured prose it was a very neat piece of villainy. An outlay of some £1200 on a furnished maisonette, some hard graft for a year as a window cleaner for one, and then the big snatch for two, and away, rich and clean.

Outside the attic window, bosomy pigeons paced the roof like gouty Grand Duchesses.

'Here it ends,' said Lynch to no one in particular 'the case that never began.'

He swung the last volume up on to the long shelf and dressed them all like po-faced Guardsmen.

If only Valerie Scott had had the nous to get shot on the day of the robbery, one might have inferred some connection, but who ever heard of a witness being murdered two months before the crime?

If only she had had the nous not to get shot at all!

He descended the crumbling staircase to a disconsolate Crisp, swinging his legs on the counter.

'Tea and fairy buns, and how to make

mobiles out of your granny's old stays. I had a belting time. How about you?'

'Too early to say. I'll be writing,' answered Lynch. 'Do you ever feel there's been a decline in reverence? Now me, I keep my granny's old stays pressed between the leaves of my calf bound volume of 'Little Women.' Thanks for your help.'

Crisp flapped a weary hand in farewell 'It wasn't a pleasure.'

Outside, Lynch made to turn in the direction of his car, hesitated, then swung round towards the High Street. Crossing at the cinema he walked down, away from the bridge, passed the Cafe Roxanne, walked on and then stopped.

The Pritchard Building was black marbled modernity in six floors, shouldering its bulk aggressively between lower, older buildings to proclaim functionality and commerce. A bus high underpass flanking the main entrance beckoned him in to a square courtyard where cars were sardined round a green fountain spraying nothing but cigarette ends and old newspapers. Three storeys up, metal bars picked out the cashier's lavatory in striped parenthesis. Cooper and friend weren't coming back; not that way, at any rate.

Outside again, he stood with his back to the Pritchard Buildings and got his bearings. Behind him and to his left was the Cafe Roxanne; opposite him and slightly to his right Trott, Chudleigh's windows squinted at him. Using the crossing outside her office, Valerie Scott must have passed the Pritchard Building at least four times a day. So what? Hundreds, thousands of people did the same. She was killed on the 15th of May and Cooper came into his inheritance on the 28th of August — ergo? Ergo nothing! But the 15th of May was a Thursday and Brace & Clelland had their windows washed every second Thursday, but did that mean the second Thursday of every month or did it mean every two weeks on a Thursday? It would be interesting to find out whether Kleenglass had operated on the Pritchard Building on Thursday the fifteenth of May. From his little experience, window cleaners' time tables were rendered flexible by season and weather. Suppose Brace and Clelland had had their panes polished on Thursday the fifteenth of May, what did it prove? Nothing! Still, it would be satisfying to know, one way or the other.

He found a telephone box and dialled the number the tattered directory showed for Kleenglass. The far off bell rang and rang, seeming to get lonelier and lonelier the longer it went unanswered. His watch said ten past six. At quarter past he conceded that Kleenglass was buttoned down for the night, and replaced the sweaty receiver. There was always tomorrow.

Back at the Staines Banner he got into the car and sat, debating, behind the wheel. He could take the road to the right and head for Datchet or he could go straight on for Staines Bridge and the 'Crusader'.

Somewhere he had read or heard that girls liked to have nights off from men, nights when they could wash their hair or press their skirts, nights when some of them could mark exercise books, or introduce themselves to Calculus. Back at the 'Crusader' he could match dram for dram with Charles in their antique duel about who could drink the most, and, incidentally, do some thinking. Some of his best had been done, incidentally, in bars.

He switched on the engine and headed resolutely for the log jam at Staines Bridge it was; he decided rather disappointedly, a night for thinking.

8

The crossword yielded five answers next morning before Lynch lit his after-breakfast pipe; he judged that the compiler must be having an off day. He went for his car about ten.

A misty drizzle had interrupted, temporarily, the long cycle of cloudless, sun-drenched days, and it accompanied him all the way to Kingston-upon-Thames, which was mouse dun, constricted, and claustrophobic.

Kleenglass was an unpainted shed sagging achingly against a down-at-heel Victorian semi-detached in the shadow of the power station. A faded sign read 'J. MORGAN, PROP.' Lynch's knock produced J. MORGAN, PROP. as if he had been lying in ambush. Thin, dark and glowering, his pencil moustache and sideburns, mourned, forever, the passing of Valentino.

'Cooper! I can tell you one thing about

him — he bloody ruined me. I had a gold mine here.'

His outflung arm embraced the El Dorado of the packed yard and the palsied lean-to.

'Four bicycle barrows, two vans and all the contract work I could handle! But now!' he spat viciously. 'The buggers round here wouldn't let me wipe their spectacles. Bloody Cooper!'

A young Indian came out of the house and bowed nervously to Morgan's stony stare. Morgan watched the slight figure retreating hurriedly out of sight, 'Lodgers! Wog Lodgers! Christ! I pissed on them during the war, pissed on them.'

'All the old values are being eroded,' sympathized Lynch, producing three crisp one-pound notes. 'I'd like to see Cooper's time-sheet for Thursday the 15th of May, 1975.'

J. MORGAN, PROP. eyed the notes hungrily, 'For three quid you can see the tattoo on my arse.'

He palmed the notes, kicked open the shed door, and switched on the light in one irate movement, 'Come into the office.'

Lynch poked his head in and quickly withdrew it. Now he knew who collected what rag-and-bone merchants threw away.

'It's a bit crowded. I'll wait out here.'

Dust billowed out of the open door as Morgan ferreted deeper.

'Everything's filed, you see,' he coughed out at Lynch. 'Once you've got the right file, you're laughing.'

Lynch said he could see that and sheltered behind an old bath tub until J. MORGAN, PROP. emerged, sanded and triumphant, waving a sheaf of grimed papers.

'Time sheets, 1975. You gotta have system in any business. What day did you say?'

'Thursday the 15th of May.'

The monarch of Kleenglass thumbed through the cob-webby bundle with the concentration of a research scientist. 'They're all here — do all my own bookkeeping, you know.' Lynch made appropriate admiring noises and spared a pang for all the deprived chartered accountants in Kingston-upon-Thames.

'Here it is — Thursday the 15th of May. Knew I could find it.'

He dusted the crumpled sheet with a dirty forearm.

'Half past eight to eleven, Finnegans, Chertsey — good money that was — the thieving bastard. Eleven thirty to one Brace and Clelland, Staines, well we know what happened to Brace and Clelland. Hm! He knocked off at one that day, must have been a race meeting that day.'

'You must have been a generous employer, Mr Morgan, letting your workers off to go racing.'

'Did I hell! Do I look like a mug? No, he would have back trouble. Had it every now and again, especially when there was racing handy. Back trouble my behind! He wasn't conning me. But what can you do? Window cleaners don't grow on trees.'

'Keen on racing, was he?'

'Horses, dogs; had a bet on every day. We got a few winners off him, come to think of it. Racing and beer. Here, feel this!'

Before Lynch could resist, his hand had been grabbed and pressed against the other's abdomen.

'Flat as a board. You never see a window cleaner with a belly, do you? Bleeding athletes we are.'

A passing shopper stopped and stared, her curlers frozen in disapproval; Lynch jerked his hand away.

'But that Cooper! Paunch on him like a pregnant woman! Three pints of Newcastle Brown every lunch hour, as if he was taking medicine, not as if he seemed to enjoy it even.'

'Sociable, was he?'

'Not so as you'd notice. Bit of a hard case, actually.'

'Any girlfriends, mates, anything like that?'

'No idea. I didn't mix with the men a lot. Well, you can't, can you!'

Lynch acknowledged the unbridgeable gap between the officers' mess and the NAAFI canteen.

'What about Grant, the one who was on the round with him? He might know what Cooper did that afternoon.'

'You'll need a medium for that, mate. Heart failure six months ago.'

For another ten minutes Lynch probed, but J. MORGAN, PROP. was wrung dry. He left him sitting on an upturned bucket, brooding over his vanished principality of portable ladders and chamois leathers.

The sun elbowed through, vanquishing the clouds, as he drove back down the A30 to saddle of mutton and Biddy's Irish coffee, prepared with the loving skill of a miniaturist.

The afternoon he spent lying under the trees again, listening once more to Frances on tape. But by the time he left to pick her up in the evening his net gain was the conclusion that she had a voice that would force nightingales to sign up for singing lessons.

'It may not be much for an afternoon's hard listening,' agreed Frances, as they drove through Gerrards Cross in search of dinner, 'but it's a great comfort to a crabbed old school ma'am. I bet your dentist scrapes his fillings off the Blarney Stone.'

Beaconsfield was rosy and placid as they relaxed in the hotel lounge, by an open window, coffee and snifters of brandy by their elbows.

'Why here?' her eyes caught his over the glass, 'I mean so particularly?'

'Chesterton. I grew up on him — Solomon and Puck in one roly-poly pudding. In a book I had there was a picture of him in his garden at Top Meadow: from Govan it looked like Samarkand, or Lyonesse, or Aschalon. When I came, eventually, it lived up to my childish visions. Not many places do, so I come whenever I can.'

Unasked, a waiter came and refilled their coffee cups and went off for more brandy.

'I wasn't any use, then, Pat, on the tape recorder?'

He shook his head.

'I've spent forty-eight hours chasing up blind alleys, sniffing red herrings and bashing my hard little head against brick walls.'

He recounted the fruitless efforts of the past two days.

'And this Fusilier Lockett could have been the sniper?'

'Could have been, but he's not telling. Willy Pascoe can't say one way or another and if Willy doesn't know, I'm not going to find out.'

'So we're stuck.'

'Stuck. There's only the airy, insubstantial Lynch hypothesis which gets us nowhere. All it does is suggest motive and motive's what has been conspicuously lacking in this case.'

He fussed with his lighter.

'Get on with it, Lynch,' she exclaimed impatiently. 'A girl could turn into an ice-maiden, sitting here — dangling.'

'Sorry! Bad bachelor habit, taking one's sweet time.'

The smoke spiralled in the sunlight.

'Two, no three months after Valerie was killed, AFTER, mark you, a building firm almost directly opposite her office was robbed of ninety thousand pounds. Remember?'

She shook her head.

'Two very, very competent villains posing as window cleaners. One of them had set the blag up by taking a job with the window cleaning firm a year before. Cooper that was. Not his real name, I wouldn't think. The other we know nothing about. The day Valerie was killed, Cooper was cleaning that same builder's windows. Also, he took that afternoon off.'

'So, what's the connection? Did he clean her windows as well? Or Trott, Chudleigh's? Or what?'

'No. Not that I know of. But suppose, as Valerie walks across the road that Thursday, she sees Cooper with bucket and leather. Did Valerie ever live or work in what is popularly known as 'The North'?'

'Never. We were both what you might call 'South orientated.' Anyway, a number of people would have seen Cooper in Staines that day.'

'Yes, but only Valerie was killed that day. What if she recognised Cooper from some context other than window cleaning, knew him in his true incarnation. Maybe she doesn't, but Cooper thinks she might have recognised him, or is afraid she might. So, three months later when there is a hue and cry for a naughty window cleaner called Cooper, Valerie pops up and says 'I know him, he's not Cooper, he's Jones who kept a whelk stall in Scarborough.' She fingers the real him from innocent milieu they have shared before 12th June, 1974.'

'Why then?'

'Because that's when not-Cooper establishes himself in the Staines area as Cooper and gets a job on the 17th of June as a window cleaner.'

'But surely, if Valerie recognised him as not-Cooper there is a chance that someone else might.'

'You ever been to — let us say Barrow-in-Furness?'

'No, nor Tobermory, nor Santa Barbara. I've never even been to Ruislip, would you believe?'

'Suppose you put on two stones in weight — '

'Heaven forbid! I'm big enough as it is.'

'Hush woman, I'm hypothesising! Suppose you put on two stones, dyed your hair red, put on dark glasses, changed your name to McGillicuddy, and got a job in Woolworths in Barrow-in-Furness, how many people would you expect to recognise you as that dishy raven haired schoolteacher Frances Gavin from Datchet?'

'Not many.'

'The odds against even one must be great.'

'But not impossible, though, if your hunch about Valerie recognising Cooper is correct.'

'Agreed. And once you eliminate that one, the odds against meeting another one who would recognise you must be even greater.'

'Perhaps. Do you really think a couple of stones would be an improvement?'

'All the better to hold you by.'

'Sorry. I'll be serious. I think your hypothesis is still way, way out. By and large we knew the same people — '

'You didn't know all the people who came into her office. She didn't know your colleagues, your pupils. But even if Cooper is someone you both knew, you weren't in Staines High Street at

1.00 p.m. on Thursday, the 15th of June, 1975, and Valerie never got a chance to mention him to you. We can assume that she didn't mention him to Bundy either, or the police would have got it out of him.'

'But wait, wait a minute you Celtic runaway. Look at your time span on the 15th of June 1975. Valerie sees Cooper between twelve and one, and she is murdered just before five on the same day. Now, that implies that Cooper knew where she lives, knew or surmised that she walked across the green, home, reconnoitred the green, found a spot to shoot from, found a rifle — '

'Or a rifleman — don't forget X.'

'But doesn't that hypothesis let Fusilier Lockett out?'

'How so?'

'Well, Cooper and X until one o'clock that day are unaware that they're going to need a rifleman. You're not going to tell me that in four hours they can advertise for a killer, get on to Fusilier Lockett at Kilburn, negotiate with him and get him down to Egham. It's just not on.'

'Sharp girl. They could have had Lockett on a retainer for all we know. Alright, alright: it's way out.'

'So we're back to X?'

'Yes indeed! Who is X? Cooper's dumb friend on the robbery, who has to be a local. He knew about Brace and Clelland, he knew about Kleenglass, a year or so before the crime. Cooper was 'imported' from the North because X would be recognised if he worked for Kleenglass around Staines. X would know Englefield Green, would know the bus routes. Cooper and X wait to see Valerie get out of work, see her get on the bus, hop into X's car for there is no evidence of Cooper having a car — another pointer to X being local and handy — then forge ahead of the bus and be up at the green in plenty of time to set the ambush and stash the car'.

Frances shuddered and stood up, 'I don't know that I could go all the way with that, but it seems to me that to prove or to disprove your hypothesis you'd have to find Cooper.'

He nodded.

'How?'

'God knows! Her father's dead, Bundy had nothing to give to the police, there's only you left, pet, so far as I can see.'

'And if I can't help?'

He shrugged, 'The police might turn up the payroll snatchers, but after two years it isn't very likely.'

They drove fast down the near empty road to Stoke Poges where, already, a few glimmering lights studded the violet afterglow. Lynch glanced sideways at the dark hair flying in the wind, the full lips parted in a half smile.

'You like fast driving?'

'Depends on who's driving. I do at the moment.'

'I remember you saying on the tape how you had to wait until Valerie dozed off before you could let the car out on the motorway; she had this hang-up about fast-driving.'

He changed down for the narrow convolutions before Slough Crematorium.

'Poor Val! She had a traumatic experience the day she passed her driving test. The instructor brought her home in the driving school car. Immediately he left, she decided to drive into work on her own. You know how it is: you're over the moon. So, she came out of that side road where she lived — bang — straight into the side of a car going down the hill, she wasn't doing above twenty, fortunately.'

Lynch sailed through two sets of green lights without slowing. 'Anybody hurt?'

'The driver of the other car lost a tooth, bled a bit, nothing serious. His mudguard was smashed in, so his car wasn't drivable, but there wasn't a lot of real damage. Of course there wasn't a soul about; there never is when you want them. But poor Val was in shock, absolutely petrified; she couldn't even drive her own car back home. The other driver had to drive them both back in her car to her place. Spitting blood and obscenities in equal amounts I gathered. He didn't put a lot of faith in women drivers it seemed. You couldn't blame him in the circumstances.'

'Who was he? The other driver?'

'I don't know. He was on his way to the

races, Ascot I suppose. I'm not sure.'

'Races, races? Friend Cooper was a great one for the races, too.'

He nipped nimbly into the run-in before her garage, 'The toothless driver and the felonious window cleaner one and the same person?'

'That connection is so slender it's practically invisible.'

'I know. But there's someone Valerie met that you never knew. Can you remember anything else about him, anything Valerie mentioned.'

'Not straight off,' she put her hand over his on the driving wheel, 'I'd have to think without distraction, if you know what I mean. I'm not sure I can remember anything more, or if there is anything for me to remember. Anyway, millions of people like racing.'

'Me, for one, and you. I know. But this is clutching at straws week. Would you know who she had her car insurance with?'

'Same company as me, Imperial Car; in fact I put her on to them; they have an office in Staines.'

'Good. See how much you can remember about the driver by lunch-time tomorrow. I'll pick you up then and buy you a bag of crisps.'

'And what will you be doing while I'm slaving away over Geometric Progressions?'

'Putting the arm on Imperial Car.'

'Will you come in and have one for the road?' her voice betrayed the faintest tremolo.

'I think not, Frances. My honourable intentions barely survived the last time.'

She got out of the car and leaned over to kiss him on the cheek; the fragrance of her hair swirled around him.

'Mine fell flat on their fat face the minute I closed the door on you — they haven't got up since.'

He kissed her palm goodnight. 'So it's all up to Pat Lynch is it? And him the spineless cratur that he is.'

'I'm afraid so.'

He backed out on to the road in a scrunch of flying stones and gunned the car away as fast as the curves would allow. If what he was feeling was tenderness then it was a hell of a time to discover it.

9

Imperial Car had two floors of a scaled down United Nations Building near the station. The manager's office was the size of a meadow, pastel tinted, trapping the morning sun. The manager, portly, pin-striped, and balding poured the coffee himself, with abstracted precision.

'Blackouts!' he repeated, with a falsetto voice. 'But we settled in full, over four years ago. Black, no sugar, you said?'

Lynch nodded.

'I think,' he lied, 'that what happened was that, shortly before he died, Mr Scott had a letter, or perhaps a telephone call, from the other party, suggesting that he was having delayed effects from the accident.'

He hoped that the Scotts, wherever they were, would forgive him.

'But you say that Mr Scott died about eighteen months ago — if there's been nothing in all that time — '

'Yes, but the estate was only settled this week — I couldn't be located you see. But I want to get everything squared away, once and for all. I suppose being Mr Scott's heir, I am his daughter's heir in a way. If there's anything in this claim I'd like to know before I take legal advice.'

'Blackouts! They keep trying it on and the courts keep swallowing it.'

He looked again through the file lying beside the coffee tray and then handed it to Lynch, 'It's all there, what there is, and it isn't much. We settled in full, hire of a car to take him to Windsor races — '

'Ascot!' corrected Lynch, unthinkingly.

The manager looked at him patiently and took a sip of coffee before replying. 'Windsor. Remember we were paying hire of a car to the races, then to take him back home to Manchester, a further three weeks till his own car was repaired, cost of repairs to his car. It's all there; no mention there of any blackouts; no medical claims at all, as a matter of fact; could hardly be if he drove himself to the races and drove himself back to

Manchester the same day. Of course Miss Scott — well 'de mortuis nisi bonum' and all that but she was very very foolish to admit responsibility to the police.'

'But she was responsible.'

'Oh, yes, not a doubt. But she tied our hands, you see, tied our hands. If people only had the sense to say nothing, absolutely nothing.'

Lynch found what he was looking for: 'Joseph Ramsden, 29, Turf Accountant, 16 Lisbon Street, Manchester'.

'Of course it will all come back to us if he does claim, and the medical grounds would have to be cast iron. But if he gets in touch with you whatever happens, say nothing. Insist he talks to us. Absolutely imperative.'

'He hasn't been in touch with you then?'

Imperial Car shook its hairless head, 'Nothing up to now. But don't forget: say nothing, refer him to me. And let me know at once if he does get in touch.'

Lynch promised, and left him, staring bleakly at the file, and the black-hearted greed of all humanity.

The 'Spinning Wheel' overflowed with oak beams, warming pans, hunting prints, and wheelback chairs.

'I know it's a bit precious,' admitted Frances, following his appraising eye, 'but it's handy and it really is home cooking. I'll have the steak pie; you have the curry: I can recommend it.'

'My blood's overheated already; do you think it would be wise?'

She smiled at him. 'Why do you think I'm having the steak pie?'

'He must have been with Valerie for about an hour at least. She bathed his cuts and made some tea. He phoned the police, and arranged for a break-down truck, and a hired car. The police came and got all the details. He went off in the hired car to Ascot.'

'Windsor. There wasn't any racing at Ascot that day.'

'Alright, Windsor. I knew it was racing.'

'Any idea what he looked like?'

She shook her head. 'Somehow I don't think he was old — late twenties or early thirties; I can't vouch for that, it's only my remembered impression from what Val said.'

Lynch scooped up his golden pudding.

'Not bad for a tottery old teacher. He was twenty-nine. I got some help from Imperial Car this morning, even though it's Saturday. Joseph Ramsden, Turf Accountant. And guess where he came from! Manchester! Remember Cooper's North Country accent.'

'But Manchester's in the Midlands.'

'I know that, you know that; but most Southerners, when they get past Watford, start looking for the woad on the natives' faces.'

'It's still very slender.'

She drank her milky coffee slowly.

'And, as far as you know, she never saw Ramsden again — unless she ran into him in Staines High Street, making like a window cleaner?'

'We don't know that she ran into anybody the day she died.'

'No, we don't. All we have is an assumption which has not yet collapsed. If the driver of the car Valerie hit had been a woman, or an old man of eighty, or a German Count, then the Barrow-in-Furness theory would have been dented. But it isn't — so far — if anything it's a little sturdier — a man of twenty-nine, Cooper was in his early thirties; a racing man; a North Country accent; known by Valerie but not by you.'

'I'll concede that it hasn't collapsed yet, but nothing else.'

Lynch paid the bill and they left the teashop. She hooked her arm in his as they strolled back to her house.

'Miss Gavin, what will your girls say if they see you with a feller?'

'They'll try and get your phone number. Eighteen year olds can be predatory as well as pretty. Why do you think I'm holding on to you like grim death.'

'You would agree that I ought to take a peek at Ramsden if I can.'

'Oh, yes, if only to eliminate him from the Lynch hypothesis.'

'But I can't do much about him till Monday, so what do you think about packing a towel and costume and spending a lazy week-end by the deep blue sea?'

'I think it's a wonderful idea except that this week-end is reserved for the Geography Field Trip which I should have been on from nine o'clock this morning, with Miss Harrison and thirty schoolgirls.'

'Why aren't you?'

'Because, totally unlike me, I forgot all about it until Miss Harrison phoned me at nine twenty this morning. She was a little put out.'

'But I thought you were Maths and Physics.'

'I am, but most of the others have kids or aged mothers or Siamese Cats so I always help Dolly out. I was firm about our lunch date, though. I said I'd join up with the party this afternoon. I am sorry, Pat.'

'No more than I. Never mind. I'll take a cold bath or find a cricket match and catch up on some sleep. Actually, it's a blessing in disguise.'

'Thank you Lynch! You're such a flatterer!'

'Cool it, teach! All I meant was that with the temptation of your beautiful bikini clad body removed I might as well drive up to Manchester tomorrow and be out with my magnifying glass first thing Monday morning.'

'You'll ring as soon as you get back.'

He laid his cheek against hers.

'What do you think?'

Impulsively, she flung her arms around him, pulled him close, then released him.

'Whatever will my neighbours think? I'd better go in and pack my rucksack. I left ten minutes ago.'

He watched the door close behind her before backing his car out. Geography Field Trips, he decided, might be all right for eager schoolgirls, but they did nothing at all for Pat Lynch. When he became Minister for Education, he would abolish them.

10

For Lynch the Public Library did for Manchester what the Eiffel Tower did for Paris and the Scott Memorial did for Edinburgh, whatever that was. When he entered the library on Monday morning, it was still doing it. He took the massive directories and the maps to a table where an acned youth in a college scarf, like a two toned winding sheet, glared at the interruption, then turned back, magnetized to his technicolour anatomy book.

'If you close it,' offered Lynch, helpfully, 'then open it at random, I'll lay you ten to one in new pence it'll always open at the same place. They all do; at least they did in my day.'

A red tide washed over the dunes and craters of the disdainful face, then the youth jumped and fled, clutching the thick tome protectively to his chest.

'Only trying to help,' Lynch called after him.

He opened the directories, oriented the street maps and settled down to pinpoint Lisbon Street.

Fifteen minutes later he was back in his car, a rough route map lying on the seat beside him.

He found Whitworth Street West easily enough, passed the Cathedral, and the Exchange Station, ducked under three bridges and then bowled sedately along Bury New Road, counting off the left hand turns as he went. Half a mile or so along he turned left, and the car bucked and curvetted on the uneven cobblestones like a frisky stallion. At the first corner he brought the bonnet round right and stopped.

Lisbon Street or what remained of it ran parallel with the main road he had just quitted. It was gap-toothed like an old skull. To his right a breach opened and widened into a salient of rubble and sickly grass, sprouting old prams, and sweeping, like a wreck strewn delta into Bury New Road. Two arthritic trees made a black V framing a distant factory.

He got out and walked along the

scarred pavement.

Twenty-four houses there had been, in two rows of twelve, facing each other — a Victorian guard of honour. Half a dozen still stood, voiceless, shunning notice. Number 4 and Number 8 were empty sockets, but Number 6 sported clean curtains and a smokey chimney. Number 10 had been surgically sliced to expose entrails of flapping wallpaper and sad old fireplaces. Lynch felt like a voyeur.

A sturdy concrete post supported a waist high iron gate bearing the number 16. It sagged open at his touch and he stepped into a shallow, brick sprinkled depression. One thing was certain: Ramsden didn't live here any more. He paused, uncertain, inside the gate: he could try the remaining houses where life still pulsed; he could wait for the postman; he could take a page in the Guardian; he could go back to Datchet; he liked the last one best.

A milk float rattled and rang on the cobbles and finally limped to a halt outside Number 6. As Lynch walked towards it, the milkman got out of the cabin and heaved down a wire basket, clanking with bottles — a spare elderly man in a striped apron, with a red peaked cap over a weathered face.

'Cream, milk or junket?'

'Gossip,' affirmed Lynch. 'Whatever happened to Number 16? Ramsden talk in his sleep?'

'Not that one. No, they're all coming down as the tenants get re-housed. Old Mrs Ramsden died a year ago, or thereabouts. You a friend of his — Ramsden?'

'Not till I know a bit more.'

The milkman put down the wire basket, pulled a blackened cigarette butt from behind his ear and lit up. It had been long years and many Government Health Warnings since Lynch had last seen anyone keep a cigarette there.

'Not much to know — lived off his old mother most of his life.'

'Not a worker then?'

'Not so as anyone would notice. Wide boy, horses and dogs — professional punter he called himself for a while, then he ran a book at the dog track for a bit but he soon got squeezed out, not enough money behind him at that time.'

'You wouldn't know what he does now or where he lives?'

'You know, the betting shops didn't make all that much difference to me. A lot of my customers are too far away from them. And then they work to a routine, housewives do — wash up the breakfast dishes, sit down and have a fag and go through the form in the paper, make their selection and then get on with the rest of the housework. Most of them don't go down to the shops till mid-afternoon.'

'So?' queried a baffled Lynch.

'So I still collect a lot of their betting slips and bring their winnings next day when there are any, and I've still got connections, and I still hear things.'

'What things?'

'Things like Ramsden making a big killing in the Ascot Gold Cup a couple of years ago and sinking it into a swank gaming club in the city.'

'What's it called?'

'You'll never believe — the Club

Lisbon — fancy calling a club after this tip. Twenty thousand they say he picked up at Ascot, but they always exaggerate.'

Lynch took a pound out of his wallet, 'I like a bit of a gamble, myself. Nobody's memory's as good as he thinks it is.'

The milkman ground the miniscule butt blackly into the cobbles, 'I'll back mine for a quid.'

'Ramsden — June, 1974 through to August 1975?'

'Inside. The old woman said he had a job in the South, but what would you expect her to say? For my money he was inside — grevious bodily harm or some such I shouldn't wonder. I know it's a guess but he wasn't here. A pint every second day for over a year then back up to three pints a day; Sonny liked his cornflakes. She died what? '76? No. Happen it was '75 — winter. He moved out, and he hasn't been back, but I hear things, like I told you.'

Lynch tucked the note into the milkman's breast pocket, 'You win — must be the open air life.'

'Nay. It's all that double cream.' He

retrieved the basket. 'Time for my tea break.'

He disappeared, whistling into the briar zareba defending Number 6, and Lynch retraced his steps to the car, started up, then switched off again. What kind of detective was it that forgot to ask what Ramsden looked like! Six foot three and red bearded and it wouldn't matter whether he had been in Staines on the 15th of May, 1975, or Stavanger, or inside, even.

He lit his pipe and reviewed what he had:

Ramsden, a racing man from Lancashire, on the way to Windsor races in 1973 is run into by Valerie Scott at Englefield Green. With him for an hour, bathes his cuts, that way you could get to remember a face.

Cooper, the window cleaner with the passion for racing, and the 'North Country' accent works for Kleenglass from June '74 until August '75.

Ramsden away from Lisbon Street for roughly the same period according to the milkman. Inside or working down

South — you took your pick.

Thursday, the 15th of May, 1975, Cooper is in Staines High Street as is Valerie Scott. At the same time? Perhaps. Valerie Scott is killed the same day. No perhaps. August '75, Cooper and X rip off Brace and Clelland. Cooper quits Staines — and the South? Perhaps. Ramsden reappears for his three pints a day and buys his club with his killing from — Ascot? Or Staines? Or Engelfield Green?

The abandoned milk float glinted cheerfully in the sun; nobody came near it. He looked at his watch: half an hour was surely enough for a tea break; it was long enough for a lot of things. He debated going to Number 6 himself and asking for Ramsden's vital statistics, but reminded himself in time that you could get your nose broken when you poked it in where it had not been invited. Besides, he hadn't been in a gaming club since the night the two constables had pulled him off Strapper: the Club Lisbon might be rewarding in more ways than one.

He switched on the engine again and

left it idling for a minute. Nothing moved; no curtain twitched in Number 6; Lisbon Street dozed away the morning, unheeding. He reversed and pointed back the way he had come. He couldn't think of anything else to do: it was going to be a long day.

11

Dinner was the high point of the hotel day — regimental, ceremonial in slow time, many coursed, liturgical. The food fell a long way short of the ritual but it served.

At nine, soothed with Armagnac, he came out and sought the chatty doorman.

'About two hundred yards, sir; not worth taking the car. Go up alongside the insurance building, take the third right and you're there.' He glanced up at a sky like dirty snow. 'Might be a bit of rain, later. You never can tell.'

Lynch agreed that you never could.

The insurance building wore a head-band of upright metal letters, reading, improbably, 'Scottish Widows'. As he turned right he had a sudden, chilling vision of battalions of Scottish Widows, their steel grey hair taut over clenched, gaunt faces, their burning, bereaved eyes boring into his back, their banshee voices screaming at him, 'Dicer, whoremaster, Papist!'

He raised two fingers at the Scottish Widows.

The Club Lisbon's blue neon flickered urgently between a smart boutique and a chic florist's. A striped awning sheltered a commissionaire in powder blue with white piping.

'Good evening, sir!' a bulging arm snapped in salute. Lynch took in the wide, unpadded shoulders and the scar tissue round the eyes, and wondered why Ramsden employed a fast cruiserweight to guard the entrance; maybe he needed to.

'Straight up the stairs, sir.'

The frescoes were bold and raw: the beach at Estoril, a street cafe in Lisbon; they hadn't come cheap. They swept him up on blue carpeted flight to a foyer of Moorish palms and ornamental wrought iron.

'Name, sir?'

Behind a long counter of studded red leather, a girl, longing to be twenty, reigned over a thick open register. White shoulders billowed voluptuously up and out from a strapless black frock. Long, fluffy, blonde hair framed baby blue eyes and a pursed red mouth.

'Pandy,' said Lynch, 'Tony Pandy.'

'That would be Anthony, would it, sir?'

'Indeed it would.'

A miniscule frown pleated the flawless brow, 'You're not a member yet, sir?'

Lynch shook his head, 'Anxious to become one, though.'

She wrote, laboriously, bending low over the register.

'Let joy be unconfined!' remarked Lynch.

'Sir?'

'Pay no attention, just boyish high spirits.'

She straightened up reluctantly and the peepshow slipped back into place.

'Three guineas, sir.'

'Worth it for the cabaret alone,' said Lynch placing the money on the counter.

'But we haven't got a cabaret, sir.'

'That's what you think, Juno my girl.'

'But my name isn't — '

The swing doors opened directly into

the club proper — a smooth conversion of an office floor into a necklace of connecting rooms. He passed from fruit machines, through roulette, chemmy and craps into a spacious bar. Somebody at a piano sent a riffle of music through the clinking of glasses and the ratchet of roulette.

He carried his overpriced whisky into a cardroom watched some very tight poker, and then wandered on to a bridge game — three bluff men of affairs and a youngish man with an intense Byronic face. He watched, at a distance, for ten minutes until the younger man and his partner counted out thirty eight pounds in front of them and got up from the table. Lynch came upsides the youngish player at the bar as he downed a double whisky in one shuddering gulp.

'You play a good game of Bridge.'

'At thirty eight pounds down in three rubbers. You must be joking.'

'Only a very imaginative player could have kept it so low. You've won a few tournaments, I would think.'

'As a matter of fact I have. I play for

the University: I teach Biology.'

'You're good; everyone says so, including me. And someone told you there's a lot of loot to be dug out of tired business men who play badly for high stakes in places like this. Yes?'

'Close enough. My name's Kirby by the way. I'd buy you a drink but — ' he threw out his hands, palms up.

Lynch ransomed two double malts from the bandit behind the bar.

'You're not suggesting there was anything crooked about the game. If I thought that I'd see this fellow Ramsden and — '

'Get your face re-modelled? Not worth it. What could you say, anyway? You came in, there were two men at the Bridge table, you asked if there was any chance of a game. They agreed, if you could find a fourth. Then this other stranger happened in, also looking for a game. Right?'

'More or less.'

'You and he, the other stranger were partners?'

'Yes. Mind you we held goodish cards,

but he wasn't — '

'Wasn't up to your standard?'

'Actually he wasn't. But don't forget he lost thirty eight pounds as well.'

'I saw the last ten minutes. Every time you had a good hand he shut down too early, very reluctantly, of course. When you held an average hand he pushed you up that little bit too high and you went down. He never gave you the best lead, only a reasonable one.'

'True. But I didn't expect him to be as good as me.'

Lynch laughed heartily. 'As good as you! He's ten times better than you or I will ever be. You were taken, Kirby, old lad, smoothly and legally. When you leave here they'll divvy up your thirty eight quid, like Caesar's Gaul, into three parts and wait for the next stranger. And there's nothing you can prove or complain about.'

'I think,' said Kirby, getting up from the bar stool, 'that you're very, very right. I might have thought it was just bad luck tonight and tried again. Thanks for the drink and the analysis. From now on I'll stick to duplicate and the pursuit of International Match Points. Goodnight.'

He headed resolutely for the exit.

Lynch picked up his unfinished drink and noticed the absence of music.

'Boy Scouts are not usually admitted,' murmured a husky voice on his other side, 'unless they show their knees.'

He turned to the woman beside him.

'He was a real tenderfoot: came out without his woggle. What would you like to drink?'

She was tall, statuesque, with silver hair swept fearlessly back from a Roman profile. Her long sleeved white blouse sported a black string tie at the collar.

'Picking me up, yet, and me old enough to be — '

Her clear green eyes met his.

'My wife?'

The severe face crinkled in a smile and, for an instant, there was a happier, younger woman, with a spontaneous gaiety.

'You're quick, sir, and kind. I'll have whatever you would buy — your wife.'

He got double brandies in balloon

glasses and followed her to an unoccupied table near the grand piano.

'You haven't been here before. I should have noticed.'

'You sound very sure.'

She gestured a graceful hand at the piano, 'From eight until two I play the music that drives the patrons back to the tables. I have time to observe.'

'You don't like what you do?'

She coaxed warmth into the goblet, 'Fifteen pounds a night, six nights a week — that I like. I have three girls at a convent school and a husband who believes that work interferes with the pursuit of happiness. He doesn't let it — much.'

On a mouth moulded for laughter the bitter lines reengraved themselves.

'Ramsden a good employer?'

'He buys when he can't do anything else. A club pianist with stamina, her you have to pay: you can't beat her into playing.'

'Like that, is it?'

'When this place opened there were two other clubs in the neighbourhood:

one was burned rather suddenly, the other was wrecked by dissatisfied customers, very wrecked. Now there's only the Club Lisbon.'

'Forceful fellow?'

'Look for yourself.'

He looked at the man, moving purposefully past the piano in the direction of the bar and recalled the police description of Cooper: 'mid-thirties, 5 feet 8 inches, stocky, collar length, black hair, thick sideboards, handlebar moustache, tinted spectacles.' This one was not impossible, at any rate. Taller, certainly, but the shoes could be built up, looked so. Mid to late thirties. Dark hair crew cut, clean shaven, but definitely jowly, as if fat had once filled the pouches; no spectacles. He wore tan slacks, a dark belted jacket, nipped in at the trim waist, over a white cashmere polo neck. V'd with a gold chain holding a florid medallion. Conscious of his figure and his gear.

Lynch tried the Staines disguise on him for size — it could fit if you pulled and squeezed a lot.

'Where's t' bloody waitress?'

North Country accent alright.

Well, what a Southerner would interpret as one, or might interpret.

The barman pointed to the door with The Gainsborough Lady silhouette: Lynch took that to mean that 't' bloody waitress' had gone to the lavatory.

'Tell her vodka and bitter lemon and not to be all neet abaht it.'

The barman nodded acquiescence, Ramsden turned and made his irascible way back and through a door marked 'Private'.

'How does he manage his diet?'

'With difficulty: he likes his packing. How did you know?'

'Oh, bitter lemon on a persona for suppin' ale, I suppose, bits of left over dewlap; figure consciousness especially: when you've always been trim and spare you never think about it.'

If Ramsden was Cooper then he was being very careful, and very dedicated to not being associated with the window cleaner of Staines, even after two years. But there was no time limit on murder and the payroll snatchers had shown themselves able to take time and care.

His companion rose, lissom for her forty odd years, 'Time to drive the lemmings. The brandy was nice.'

She squeezed his shoulder, 'Ramsden's got two Jags and a padded silk sty at Alderley Edge; I've got my girls; you hang on to whatever you have and don't meddle with him. I'll play something for you — from way back, like me.'

She improvised thoughtfully and delicately for a minute or so, searching, then she stole, on sure tiptoes, into 'Manhattan', the pulse of youth and first love, as it was — way back. Wryly, he remembered his own 'Isle of Joy' — the grey ribbed town, suddenly burnished with the glow of two children's new discovered rapture in each other. He was sure she was happy in her big, big house in Bearsden but perhaps she too, was suddenly caught, hand on throat, by the echo of a half forgotten song. Probably not, she'd be far too busy living the here and now and enjoying it with Alistair or Ian or Sandy or whatever the lucky man's name was. Sensible girl!

The pianist finished to a scatter of applause and waved; he raised his glass in salute. As he made his way out past the blonde lollipop and her 'Goodnight Mr Pandy', the piano lady swept with bravura into a pounding cha-cha-cha; he hoped her three little girls deserved her.

'Taxi, sir?' the commissionaire palmed his cigarette with the leger-de-main of an old sweat on fatigues. 'A touch of rain.'

Lynch declined and made his damp way back to his hotel.

The telephone booths in the lobby were roomy confessionals for the secrets of the well-heeled. He sat in a padded armchair and dialled the Club Lisbon.

'I have a personal call for Mr Ramsden from Kingston-upon-Thames. Will he accept the call?'

'Oh, I don't know — hold on!'

He was sure he could hear the liberated bosom massaging the red leather counter; he thought he was fast becoming a dirty old man, and enjoying it.

'Ramsden here. Who is it?'

He had been quick but then personal

calls have an aura of disaster and sudden death.

'Kleenglass Window Cleaners, Kingston-Upon-Thames. I thought we might talk a little business.'

'I have a contract already, a local one.' The voice was watchfully neutral.

'You surprise me, Cooper, I mean Ramsden, I thought you might have kept your hand in.'

'What the hell are you after?' not so neutral now.

'The good life, Cooper Ramsden, the good life! You have it; I want a piece of it. There's enough for all — '

'I don't know what your bloody game is but you'll get nowt from — '

'Blackmail, Cooper Ramsden. Pure and simple blackmail, well simple, anyway.'

'I want you to keep talking, just keep talking till the police trace you, that's all.'

Lynch laughed uproariously through the telephone, 'Ramsden, the indignant honest citizen! You're a reet card, Ramsden. You could revive music hall with that act. Hey! That's a thought!

When you sell the club, why not try the stage?'

'Sell the club? You're mad! Bloody mad, that's what you are!'

'You can't stay here, Ramsden. Surely you can see that. You won't risk me coming back for seconds. Of course, I'll swear blind that this is a once and for all bite, but you won't believe me; you daren't. So, you'll sell up, disappear from Manchester and be Winterbottom, or Openshaw, or Cooper, someplace else.'

'You won't be so bleeding cocky when the panda car arrives — '

'You wouldn't be able to sell in under three weeks, if that. So, you're going to have to buy time. I'll give you three days, three clear banking days that is. Today's Monday, so we'll discount today. You have Tuesday, Wednesday and Thursday.'

'You'll give me — '

'Listen good, Ramsden. I'll only give you your instructions once. On Friday morning at eight o'clock you'll go to Runneymede — '

'I'll go where?'

'Runneymede, Ramsden, you washed a few windows around there in your day, I bet. Damp Northern air doesn't agree with me, gets on my chest, as they say. So you'll have to come to me. When you park your car you'll walk up to the Kennedy Memorial, reaching it at exactly eight a.m. I'm a stickler for punctuality. Don't interrupt. When you get there you'll find a paved path on the right. Walk along the path until you come to a stone bench. In front of it there is a little paved terrace. If it's dry, you sit on the bench. If it's wet, you sit on the bench. You'll have with you a white paper carrier bag, and in the carrier bag will be four thousand one pound notes.'

'In a pig's arse — '

'When you have sat for five minutes, no more, no less, you'll get up leave the carrier bag under the bench, with the money still inside, and start walking back down. It doesn't matter if you look back: you won't turn into a pillar of salt. But whatever you do don't stop walking down. I hope you've got all that, because if you don't do as I've told you then I'll shop you. It'll take me a few minutes to reach a phone but you can expect to be shopped about twenty past eight for Brace and Clelland.'

He put the phone down abruptly. That was it — the only throw of the dice he was going to get. And, as he saw it, this particular dice had only three faces. The first showed Ramsden as Ramsden, never Cooper, innocently working as a Bingo caller or a lady's maid in Brighton from June, '74 through to August '75, and now reporting a mad telephonist to the local nick. The second face showed Ramsden as Cooper, but sitting tight and defying anyone to prove it, including Lynch. Except that it just might be provable. And the third face, the one he was hoping would turn up, showed Ramsden as Cooper, carrying out Lynch's instructions, buying time and silence in the hope that Lynch would expose his carotid artery, just for a moment. By Friday he might know.

At Reception he settled his account and arranged an early morning call. Then he took a half bottle of Hennessey's and a paperback up to his room and settled down for the night. He hoped Ramsden had had the good sense to ring his partner, X, in the South: a trouble shared is a trouble halved.

12

Next morning the same chatty porter was standing outside by his car, cheerful despite the dawn chill.

'Half past five, sir, as ordered. Nippy, but no rain yet. Thank you, sir. No, it wasn't any trouble, really; I am an early riser.'

Traffic was light and he was on the M6 in twenty minutes, settling down to a steady seventy.

By seven-thirty the major part of the journey was achieved and his stomach was firing distress rockets. He placated it with breakfast at a near deserted service area, and was back on the Motorway just after eight, tissue and tank refuelled.

At Denham the traffic slowed, ran viscous and jammed so it was getting on for nine when he reached Staines. At the end of The Causeway he took the left hand exit by the hotel and drove along, slowly, until he found the sign he was looking for: 'Launches for Hire. By the Day or the Week'. He turned right into the boatyard.

'Give us a chance,' protested the manager. 'We haven't even started on all the stuff that came in last night. Everything's got to be inspected, cleaned-up, re-stocked. The only possibility is that big Birchwood. I could have it ready by one o'clock, half past. But it's really too big and expensive for just one person.'

'I'm going into town to do some shopping. I'll be back in one hour.'

He pushed two tenners across the counter.

'Bonus for the men who're going to have it ready when I come back. I'm not taking her on to the Western Approaches. All I want to do is find a quiet spot where I can drop anchor and work for a few days without interruption. I'll pay in advance for four days' hire.'

'Till Friday? Work?'

'I'm a writer,' improvised Lynch. 'I can't get the ending to come out, somehow, got to work at it. I'd want to leave my car here in case I have to rush back for a reference book, or a ballpoint pen or something.'

'One hour,' promised the manager.

Some eighty minutes later the 'Mary Hoy' was moving cautiously upstream. She was big enough to be handled with caution by Lynch, whose boatmanship, never more than showily superficial in his younger exhibitionist days, had rusted away to vanishing point. A thirty five footer, laminated glass fibre hull, with spacious fore and aft cabins, and, most important for his purpose, a high centre enclosed wheelhouse with curtains and sliding windows.

He found a more comfortable perch on the adjustable helmsman's seat and moved the steel rimmed steering wheel experimentally; she answered immediately. He concentrated on the dash board and ticked off again on his mental clip board the various instruments. With a three foot draught, he didn't think he was going to need the echo sounder.

When the Magna Carta Memorial showed up in the port window he slowed up, edged finically over to the Middlesex bank, touched the Morse reverse control, and brought the vessel abeam of a concrete landing stage. She nuzzled the bank and Lynch switched off. He jumped on to the landing stage, attached the painter to a bollard, and secured her aft with another line to an iron ring. He didn't know the form about using someone else's landing stage, but he knew that boat people were generally helpful to other boat people. If the owner was tetchy, Lynch would have to have an engine failure and be a distressed mariner.

For the moment there was no sign of any owner.

He climbed back on board, drew the curtains partway across the port windows of the wheelhouse, took the Zeiss binoculars out of his holdall and trained them on the car park. The registration numbers leaped at him. There had been no time to haggle with the secondhand dealer over the binoculars but they justified their £50.

His line of sight up to the Kennedy Memorial was clear and unimpeded.

There was nothing to do now but wait. The sun moved slowly round; clouded over; it began to rain.

He wondered about Ramsden: he could have driven through the night in one of his Jags, been told to.

His glasses picked out a rain-coated figure moving down from the Kennedy Memorial, he brought it into focus: a woman in slacks, a bedraggled spaniel trailing her.

Even if Ramsden hadn't yet arrived, what about X? He could be stalking the killing ground already. X — the local man, Johnny-on-the-Spot, if Lynch was right. And how would Lynch recognise him if he did come. It was all right gambling that X wouldn't arrive sans Ramsden, but he had lost money gambling before now.

What if nobody came at all?

By midday the sky was grey and sodden and the rain had set in for the day, steel spikes raking the meadow clean of people. Occasional cars crept into the car park and solitary drivers munched sandwiches, drank out of flasks, and sullenly threw crusts into the river, maligning rain, authority, and the whole damp, dripping universe. The birds sat silent on the trees behind, long-suffering, accepting, hoarding their music against a drier tomorrow. At intervals a lonely launch chugged past, hermetic, introverted. The day scowled.

Lynch, his juices battened down, sipped whisky without savour, and glumly tore his 'wild surmise' into tatters. Ramsden was just Ramsden, a lucky punter, lining his Northern stall, nothing more. Cooper and X were only shadows long melded back into the Smoke, never to be conjured up again, except by the dull incantation of police procedure. And Lynch? What was Lynch? A self deceiving, Saturday night optimist, fancying his chances against the sinewy cerebrations of those two-legged blood-hounds, Gibb and Mathews. A Celtic blowhard, conning nobody but himself!

It was that sort of day.

The deadening mirk resurrected another long ago lowering day, with a smaller Lynch, shivering on a damp groundsheet, in a dripping bell tent, his bare knees blue, while, outside, a spongy Akela tried to tease flame out of damp, green shoots. O Baden Powell, what misery was wrought in thy name!

Here at least he was cupped in comfort, lapped in proof spirit. He stirred himself from his gloom and rummaged through a pile of priapic paperbacks left by some previous sailing master, and overlooked by the cleaners and restockists. Garish covers with pneumatic bosoms and hinted pudenda — the Royal Yacht Squadron would be horrified. Then, gold among the dross! An Anthony Price he hadn't read, a nun in a whorehouse. The day was not totally lost. He poured the dross overboard, pulp to pulp, topped up his glass, sat down facing the Memorial just in case, and introduced himself to 'Our Man in Camelot'.

He sat there all day, moving only for quick snacks, his eyes never long averted from the hill opposite.

Only when the dusk trickled down like dirty water and headlights bounced off the glistening road did he come off watch.

In the forward cabin he laid out the tins

and packets he had scooped up hurriedly in the Egham supermarket, uncorked the new bottle of Talisker, tucked away the beer in the fridge in the end of the dinette seat and started the evening meal. Tinned steak, Stilton, and instant coffee followed by good whisky.

The 'Mary Hoy' swayed rhythmically in the current, bats squeaked eerily along Hythe End on his starboard, tyres swished by on the road on the far bank, the sound bouncing clean off the water. He ate slowly, and gradually the tension drained out of his neck and shoulders.

After dinner, he cleared up, briskly, made his preparations for the next day and retired to the aft stateroom, with a generous night cap. The double berth was soft and inviting and he sank gratefully into it. The last drops of whisky were warm and soporific. He turned off the bed-head light, drew back the curtains and let the rocking river take over. He had had a full day.

13

They came at twenty to eight the next morning. Which was a sensible time. They would see the conditions that they could expect to meet on the following Friday, at around eight o'clock. If there were any dogs being walked on Wednesday morning it would be reasonable to expect them giving a repeat performance at about the same time on Friday. If you jogged, you jogged daily, just as you commuted and worked. Sensible. But then he had never thought he was dealing with idiots, if he was dealing with the pair who had knocked off Brace and Clelland. And if he wasn't dealing with the pair who had knocked off Brace and Clelland, then he was enmeshed in a happening so surrealistic that the most constructive thing he could do would be to lie face down on the ground and scream his head off.

His inbuilt alarm clock and the first

preliminary tuning up from the dawn chorus had summoned him at the first glimmer of morning. He was sure he was on watch much too early, but not absolutely, so he had shaved, washed and dressed and made breakfast. Then he had filled a flask with coffee for what might be another long frustrating day ahead, and made a pile of corn beef sandwiches: cooking smells carried across water, like sound, he fancied. The curtains on the port side he had drawn to leave only a crack of daylight in the wheelhouse window. After he had finished with the rations, he had drawn the curtains on the starboard side: he didn't want any light coming in behind him. Then he had sat in the helmsman's seat, sucking an empty pipe, and peering through the portside crack, and sat, and sat.

The car came in from the Windsor side. He heard it turn off the road into the car park, roll round slowly, then reverse towards the river; suddenly the red lights were coming towards him, and then the engine stopped and the lights died. The early morning rushed back into the vacuum — the whirr of an oncoming moped, the sudden thunder of a jet at London Airport, a dog barking high up on Priest's Hill. He could see the car quite clearly, a black Aston Martin. He dared not risk the binoculars yet.

For five long minutes there was no sound or movement from the car, then, simultaneously, two men climbed out and stood on either side of it, their backs towards him, scanning the ground rising up across from, and ahead, of them. The one on the left, wearing a green windcheater and dark trousers, and carrying a white paper carrier bag, had the heft and outline of Ramsden. The driver was bigger, a nail paring over six feet, bulky, dark hair thinning over a pink tonsure. He wore a brown open-necked shirt, flowering to a yellow polka-dot cravat, tailored cavalry slacks. His left hip supported a brown canvas fisherman's bag, and his right shoulder bore the weight of a matching canvas cylinder from which protruded two fishing rods. He dragged deeply at a cigarette as he contemplated the view.

Swiftly, unexpectedly, the driver about turned and faced the 'Mary Hoy'. Lynch tightened and steeled himself to remain stock still. He saw a swarthy, full, face with a thin black moustache, a pronounced widow's peak, a dusting of white talc over a close shaven, blue chin — an alert, decisive face. The binocular case swung with him and thumped to rest on the broad, channel swimmer's chest.

Half turning he called over his shoulder to his companion, 'Handy spot to drop anchor!'

In the still thin traffic the Public School voice carried easily through the open windows of the aft cabin.

The other turned, confirming himself Ramsden, and looked at the cabin cruiser, indifferently, 'Handy for what?'

The driver's smile was wolfish, 'Precisely!'

He moved right up to the water's edge and probed the boat with his eyes, 'Heavy sleepers!'

Ramsden shrugged, and turned back to Runneymede, 'Bloody early, remember.'

Lynch held himself rigid.

X was the C.O., and a good one — wary, careful, suspicious.

He turned back to join Ramsden. Lynch stayed in his own vice. A yard short of Ramsden, X turned again, sharply, and combed the 'Mary Hoy' once more, taking his time. X was VERY good. Apparently satisfied, though Lynch wouldn't have risked an each way bet on it, he swung round and touched Ramsden's arm.

'Let's get on with the fishing then.'

Ramsden laughed 'Aye, let's see what we can catch.' The North Country accent was strong and positive.

Lynch let them get well across the grassy apron below the Memorials, before he reached for the glasses, well smeared with black tobacco ash the night before. The registration number expanded miraculously in his vision. He jotted it down on the pad on his knee, laid the binoculars aside. Though he had blacked them out thoroughly he had had to leave a clear circle in each lens to see through, and one little flash would be enough for X. Reaching for the overflowing ashtray, he smeared his nose, brow, cheeks, chin, making his face black, matt: X's glasses would be the very best available; of that Lynch was very sure. In the sparkling clear light every object was three dimensional, sharp edged, even without the glasses.

The two men had stopped at the Kennedy Memorial and were looking around, acting casual. Then Ramsden walked along to the bench, and sat down, with the carrier bag between his feet. X moved left, in the direction of the Magna Carta Memorial, plunging into the trees. From time to time he reappeared briefly as he circled around and above Ramsden. Once Lynch caught a glimpse of him, seeming to throw himself down in the prone firing position, but he could have been mistaken, it was only a fleeting glimpse.

It took him a painstaking half hour to beat the ground above Ramsden. By this time, cars had multiplied on the road below, but if the two were aware of it they weren't letting it affect their concentration. X came down, joined Ramsden, spoke, gesturing, then moved left and below, to eight o'clock in the trees. Ramsden waited, looking fixedly at his watch then moved up into the trees behind, leaving the white carrier bag at the bench. A moment later he re-emerged and walked steadily down to the bench and the carrier bag, bent down, straightened up and returned to the trees on a different bearing, re-appeared and came back down to the carrier bag, bent down straightened up again. He enacted the same scene six times, on a different axis each time, a human pencil on a compass touching six points on the upper half circle. Then he went down hill and repeated the performance on the lower half circle. X put a lot of preparation into his work.

At last, rehearsals seemed to be over for the day: the two men joined each other at the bench. X pointed down in what seemed to be the direction of the 'Mary Hoy' and focussed his binoculars on it. Of course the crack in the curtains was too small for him to see anything, and of course his nigger minstrel blacking up prohibited any reflection, but he still felt his stomach muscles contract as he stayed motionless lest the slightest movement signal his sentry go.

'You don't like us being on exactly this spot,' Lynch said inside his head, 'and I don't blame you.'

The binoculars shifted over the cruiser and to the right, picking out the substance of the house and gardens behind Lynch. The house and gardens to which, Lynch assumed, the landing stage belonged. He hoped X and Ramsden assumed it, too. For, if you have a mooring on the river, what more natural and innocent than to have a boat tied to it, your boat? Else why have a mooring at all? And so on, and so on.

But, if you have to keep on reassuring yourself, then you must have something to frighten you in the first place. So Lynch yanked out that which was frightening him and had a look at it — that X saw the motor cruiser for what it was, a forward observation post, a floating spyglass. And if he did? Then he would also see ways of taking it out. Did fibre glass burn? Lynch didn't know; he didn't want to find out either.

What if they called in at the boatyard? Then the name of the well known novelist which Lynch had assumed would not distract X from the coincidence of someone hiring a boat to take to the same place that Ramsden had been ordered to — within a few hours of his having been so ordered. And his car was at the boatyard, but that would only lead back to the car hire firm and then the bank, and stop there. But a car could be stalked, and the person in it and — X had lowered the glasses and was signalling to Ramsden, who retrieved the carrier bag. Together they began, unhurriedly, to descend the green slope — two sporting gentlemen on pleasure bent.

When they reached their car X gave the boat one swift hunter's appraisal to check that nothing had changed, the assured shikari who took his tiger in his own time; then they both climbed in, the car thundered into life and sped off in the direction of Staines.

When the last reverberation had died

away, Lynch stood up from the helmsman's chair and moved to sit down in the U-shaped settee; he did not touch the curtains. He knew what he would probably do now, if he were X. He looked at his watch — nine a.m. — he had time for a cup of coffee; he unscrewed the top of the flask, poured himself one, drank it, steaming hot though it was, then poured himself another and drank it just as quickly. He had made two mistakes at the boatyard; leaving the car was the first one but he couldn't have avoided that one and still set up watch as early as he had. But the second one! He could hear the correct establishment voice in polite query: 'And for how long did my friend hire your boat, sir? Ah, FOUR days! Back on Friday. Quite.'

One lived with one's mistakes; he hoped he was going to live with that one. At nine-thirty his ear picked up the distinctive note of the Aston Martin returning, slowing down, easing right, crunching into the car park. Lynch sat where he was making like a deserted boat, he hoped. Nobody got out of the car. He could feel them, sitting there in the driver's seat, their eyes raking over and through the drawn curtains, willing him to move, rock the boat, show a leg, sneeze loudly, cough, get a cramp, dance a jig — anything that might harden or dissolve their suspicion. They'd have a long wait. The Lynches had always liked to stay alive as long as they could, and a fig for death wishes.

Eventually, he heard the car start up again, reverse, glide on to the roadway and make off towards Old Windsor. He stole a look at his watch — twenty minutes — they must be into Yoga or Trascendental Meditation to be able to sit that long just staring at a boat. He'd have to borrow their mantra sometime.

He decided to have a smoke before doing anything else: his nerve ends needed brushing down. Then he remembered another old military saw: 'Time spent on reconnaissance is seldom wasted.' X must have been a hell of a soldier but Lynch had put in some service too. He peered through the gap in the curtain; because you heard a car drive away didn't mean that someone hadn't been let out of it very quietly. The car park was empty but for a hoody crow picking greedily around the litter bin. X hadn't left a rearguard.

It might be that he was worrying over much, investing X with too much percipience and capability; it might be; but somehow he didn't think so. He thought it might be a good thing to take out the observation post before someone else did. A car pulled into the car park and a middle aged couple got out with a lunatic King Charles spaniel on a tangled lead. Runneymede was coming to life.

Lynch pressed the starter and the engine fired immediately. He brought her about in a slow careful curve and sailed back the few hundred yards to the boatyard. His cruising days were over.

The boatyard manager was apologetic. 'You couldn't really expect a refund, now, could you? You did say four days and I've refused a couple of bookings this morning already.'

Lynch agreed that he couldn't really expect a refund, and pointed out, mildly, that he hadn't raised the subject at all.

'I know you didn't but it makes me feel bad. You know and I know that at this time of the year I'll have it out on hire again before lunch. Tell you what, since you've been such a good customer what do you say to fifty quid. It'll make me feel better.'

Lynch said that it would make him feel better too and directed him to make the cheque out to cash.

'You finished it then? Your book? You were having trouble with the ending.'

'Everything worked out — better than I thought it would. No place like the river. Did my agent track me down?'

'Agent? I'm sorry.'

'He always breathes down my neck at a time like this, when I have to meet a publisher's deadline. I tell him he only puts me off, but he likes to stand over me waiting for the last full stop. Always finds me too. I thought he might have been here asking for me.'

'No, nobody's asked for you. I assure you.'

'If he does, don't give me away, I'd like

to do this again with my next book. Works wonders.'

'Don't worry, sir, I won't. I know a good customer when I see one.'

He pocketed the cheque, transferred his gear to the car and drove out; he waited before driving onto the main road until there was no traffic coming from either direction. He stopped short of the roundabout, pulled over and got out to have a look: it was a good place to plant a watcher. There were no stalled cars or idle newspaper readers; everything was frantic — normality ruled. It didn't look as if Ramsden and X were on to him.

He followed the sign for Bagshot.

14

Lynch placed the big cardboard box tenderly down on the counter, being careful to keep the cellophane window face down.

'Can I help you?'

The clerk was in his twenties with longish, mousy hair, wearing a shirt with a fleur-de-lys motif, and a tie full as a bursting cauliflower. Lynch hoped he had made the right choice of collaborator: he was pinning his faith on that tie.

'I have the registration number of a car. I understand you may be able to give me the owner's name and address.'

'If we were satisfied that you had good reason for it — say a hit and run accident, though the police would usually be involved in that.'

'You'll have to be the judge.'

The clerk frowned in annoyance and looked at the clock on the wall — half past eleven.

'Past coffee time and too early for lunch,' sympathised Lynch, 'but this won't take long.'

The drumming fingers suggested it had taken too long already.

'I was parking just off Bond Street about four o'clock yesterday afternoon and, just as I was about to put in my money, a man came to get into the car in the bay in front of me. About my age. He was carrying this box.'

The clerk eyed the box, unmoved.

'He was just opening the door by the kerb to put it in the passenger seat, when a woman called from the other side of the street, 'John, Darling,' she cried, 'whatever are you doing in this part of town?''

''Had to see a client,' he says.'

''Lovely!' she says, 'we can have tea and I'll come home with you, save me scrambling for the train.''

Lynch's audience shuffled its feet, restlessly, 'Sir, this sounds like the beginnings of a great new radio serial, but — '

'Wait!' enjoined Lynch, 'Wait till I tell

yez! Well our friend was a bit discommoded, as you might say, but he was equal to the situation — he could read the game alright. 'Good idea, darling!' he shouts across the roof of the car, 'but my time's nearly up on the meter, we'll pick up some tea on the way home.' And with that he bends down and slips this box underneath the car, quick as a wink he was. Then he goes round, joins the lady coming across the road to meet him — acted like a wife she did, you know how they do, well no, maybe you don't. Anyways, they get into the car and drive off and there was this box lying in the road in front of me.'

His listener was webbed into the narrative now, 'What's in it?'

Lynch turned over the box and showed him: the lingerie lustrous through the cellophane, a frou-frou of sheer black with pink bows, wispy pants, slip, matching brassiere.

'Wow!' the clerk was shaken. He looked at the name on the box, 'Not much change out of a hundred quid there — '

He looked at Lynch knowingly 'Girl friend?'

'Maybe. Maybe not. The wife lady was slim enough. Could have been a surprise birthday gift, he gets a bit flustered, acts on the spur of the moment, might well be kicking himself, this very minute. Well, what would you have done? I couldn't leave it lying there. I took the number of the car before it went out of sight, picked up the box, and here I am.'

'You should take it to the police, give them the number. That's the correct thing.'

'And then what happens? Some callous old desk sergeant rings up, 'We've got your knickers down here at the station, missus.''

'And our friend's right in it.'

'Up to his collar stud, poor sod,' agreed Lynch, quickly joining the freemasonry of men of the world, 'especially if the size is wrong and she likes wool next to the skin.'

'Combinations yet. What did you have in mind, sir?'

'Give him a ring, find out what he'd

like done. Give the box to 'War on Want' if that's what he'd prefer. All very discreet.'

The young man gazed enviously at the box which Lynch had bought an hour previously in the only out of town branch of a name young women breathed in their orisons.

'Expensive car, I bet.'

'Aston Martin, this year.'

'Jammy bastard!' he whispered appreciatively. 'Still you couldn't expect that lot to be happy in a Morris Minor. Wouldn't look right, if you know what I mean. Your age you said, sir?'

Lynch nodded.

'Nice to know that people of your age are still — er — ' he fished around for an inoffensive euphemism but couldn't find one.

'Getting it?' finished Lynch equably. 'It is. Gives a young man hope for the future.'

Lynch pushed the scrap of paper across the counter.

'I'll have to phone Swansea, of course, everything's in a state of flux these days.'

Lynch put his hand in his pocket but the clerk waved him away, and winked at the same time. 'We'll have this one on the firm.'

He pointed to the box. 'Should turn that over, if you don't mind, sir. Some of the old ones here'll get hot flushes.'

Lynch complied; he was getting hot flushes himself, just looking.

In five minutes the young man returned, triumphant, and pushed the paper back across the counter.

'What'll you do if he doesn't want them? You got anybody in mind yourself, sir?'

'That's the only place I've got anybody. Could become a fetishist, maybe. What about you?'

'Haven't got an Aston Martin to go with them.' He sketched ample curves in the air, 'No. Mine's a big girl. That lot wouldn't cover her — well, good luck anyway, sir. Hope it works out.'

He turned away to the next suppliant. Lynch went out to the car park with the box under his arm.

He waited in the car park for about

twenty minutes. Then a much labelled down-at-heel Volkswagon shot in and came to a sticky halt, a few cars away. A drab girl got out, with thick spectacles, stained sweater, scuffed jeans, and made for the Motor Taxation Office, brandishing a sheaf of documents. Lynch waited until the building swallowed her before he got out, looked furtively all around, and tossed the box through the open window into the back seat. She looked as if she could do with a frisson in her life, and, so far as he could judge on such limited acquaintanceship, the cup size was right.

He got out of the car park as fast as possible: a magistrate might construe his generosity as a lewd and improper suggestion.

It was after one when he made the 'Crusader' and Charles poured immediately he saw him.

'My gear still in the trunk room?'

Charles nodded, 'Biddy'll give you the key.'

'After lunch, no hurry.'

He enjoyed lunch, but he did not dwell too long over it; he had things to do.

The trunk room had been the gun room in spacious, private days — high ceiling, wooden panelling, racks, glass fronted cases, antlers and deer heads with little name plates. In one corner rested the worldly goods of one, Patrick Aloysius Cameron Lynch, undisturbed since he had gone down, an army officer's black tin box, with the legend 'Major Lynch, D.S.O.' stencilled in bold white letters across the lid. One of these days he would have to have that particular piece of ostentation, or nostalgia, or pride, painted out. Or perhaps he wouldn't, it had been hard to come by.

He took the tin trunk up to his room and locked the door. Everything about the Crusader was expansive, he thought, as he spread newspaper thickly over the broad bedside table, the food, the grounds, the furniture. That was Biddy, he supposed, creating a suitable frame for her sheer abundance. From the trunk he took out the chamois wrapped Colt Police Special and the carton of cartridges he'd won from Towser Foran all those years ago. Not that he'd wanted a hand gun, an unlicensed, illegal immigrant, worth six month's 'bird' if found in his possession, but what could one do with a gambler like Towser when the fever was on him, and you had stripped him clean.

He could see the caravan now, aswirl with smoke, sweat, whisky fumes, the dawn stealing in from the silent fair-ground around it, Lynch's full house flat on the table, the pile of notes by his right hand. The other three had pulled back from the table, divorcing themselves from Lynch's unbeatable streak, only Towser staying in, his little fighter's face tense, pleading.

'Wait, Pat, wait! I've got something. Good as money — better — going up all the time — worth a century.'

He had gone behind the partition, returned, unwrapped the bundle on the card table.

'What the hell do I want with a shooter, Towser?' he had asked.

'An investment, Pat, an investment, like stamps; cartridges too; untraceable, I give you my word. You'll get a hundred, a hundred and fifty in that pub down New

Cross. My luck's changed, you'll see. Give me fifty now and I'll buy it back from you in an hour. I can feel it: I'm going to take you this time.'

What could you do? The strict unwritten code of machismo insisted that you let the little man go the distance until he was flat on the canvas, even though you and he knew it was hopeless. That was how he had always fought, Towser, in the half lit, sleazy halls, the bloodied booths, all the way, giving everything he had. Never beaten until he was nailed to the floor, unconscious.

And Lynch had kept the money — and the gun. An embarrassment. Until now.

He took the cleaning kit out of the flannel covering, laid it out on the newspaper, and stripped the gun down. He found he was clumsy; labouring on the Motorway did not give hands the delicacy of a surgeon. He spent a long time cleaning and oiling, not so much because the weapon needed it, but because he needed time to think. He checked the action, sighted the empty gun through the open window at a stately strolling peacock, squeezed the trigger, sighted again at a magpie in flight, squeezed. What he needed was range time, a couple of years at least.

Eventually, he put the gun and the ammunition into his holdall. He had never envisaged using it in anger, never wanted to, but with X around he would need all the edge he could get. He put the cleaning kit back in the tin trunk, locked it up and returned it to the trunk room, then took the key back to Biddy.

'What do you mean, no dinner? No dinner for nearly a week, no you either. Something wrong with the grub?'

'The grub, like you, Biddy, is rich and rare, caviare to the general, ambrosia for hungry archangels, but tonight I have to work. If you would leave two bottles of Guinness in my room and a sandwich or two, I might be late.'

'Work!' jeered Biddy. 'Some little piece with her mini up to her bum, more likely. It's time you settled down, Pat Lynch, and had a couple of kids to comfort you in your old age. And that's not so far away as you'd like to think.'

'I know, Biddy, I keep telling myself the same thing, and then along comes some little piece with her mini up to her bum.'

'It's a crate you'll be wanting tonight,' she grumbled, 'not two bottles. Bloody men! Chasing till they die.'

Back up in his room he spread out his maps on the bedside table and smoothed out the scrap of paper he had brought back from the Vehicle Licensing Office; 'Smith-Heritage, Raphael, 32 Blythswood Drive, Sunningdale.' Poncy name! He thumbed through the West Thames telephone directory; the poncy name was there, alright, with some not so poncy additives: 'Smith-Heritage, Lt.Col., C.B., M.C., 32 Blythswood Drive, Sunningdale.' So X was the soldier Lynch had taken him to be. X was the C.O. in fact. He pored over the map; but Sunningdale is hardly a congested area, or a blighted back-to-back slum; they have room to swing their Siamese and their Blue Persians; he found Blythswood Drive easily. It debouched from the Ascot Road, swung round in a long irregular crescent and rejoined the road nearer Ascot. The map declared the houses substantial, the gardens spacious; the stockbroker belt has lebensraum.

He replaced the directory and folded up his maps. Then he showered and changed into lightweight slacks, blue tennis shoes, black sweatshirt. He took the map and the binoculars down to the car and found Biddy again, invoices and accounts strewn like a carpet of autumn leaves around her at the kitchen table.

'Tradesmen! Add a little bit here, a little bit there. Thieving bastards all of them, I kid you not, Pat. The flask's in the usual place; biscuits in the tin.'

He filled the thermos from the coffee pot on the hob, put some chocolate biscuits in a paper bag, and planted a kiss on the nape of her neck.

'Promises. Always promises!'

As he reached the door she turned her head. 'Pat!'

He stopped and glanced round.

'Take care. Don't get beaten up, or nicked, or anything daft. You watch it.'

'I'll watch it, love. You know me — old

cowardy cowardy custard Lynch.'

He went out past a coven of gnarled, ancient beldames, their nostrils twitching for afternoon tea.

15

Sunningdale was only a hop, step and jump down the A30 and Lynch was there in under quarter of an hour. Blythswood Drive ran up a slight incline as it arched right, through the hedges and mini copses of the flanking gardens. The houses lay well back from the road, insulated from traffic and each other by space and leafage. Number 32 was a trimmed down Elizabethan manor house, white plaster, black timbers, with a gravelled drive curling round a lawn you could lay a snooker frame on. As Lynch eased past he could see the Aston Martin parked outside the front door; there was no sign of Ramsden's reputed Jaguars.

'Raphael Smith-Heritage is at home; bullet proof vests will be worn,' he muttered wryly to himself.

Past the gates of Number 38 and out of sight of Number 32 he pulled up. In his mirror a Bentley Continental glided majestically into Number 36. From 34 he could hear the shouting and splashing of children in a swimming pool. Summer in Arcady!

The trouble about surveillance, he decided, was that you never had your Water Board Inspector's uniform on you when you needed it, nor your gaily striped telephone engineer's tent, for that matter. Usually, you just sat in your car, as he was doing now, pretending to fill in salesman's order books, or read a map. Except that at the moment he wasn't surveilling anything except cypress. Surveilling? Was there such a word? One thing in his favour was the privacy that the residents bought with their half acres. No one was likely to spot his car from behind a twiching front room curtain.

He got out and walked back along the boundary screen of Number 32 until he found a tiny peephole between rhododendron and birch revealing the front door, a sparkling ground floor window, the bonnet of the car. He couldn't think of anything else to do but watch, so he just stood there, his open map dangling by his side ready for burying his face in if anyone came near. Nobody did. It seemed as if he had the Drive to himself.

When ten minutes had gone by, the front door of Number 32 opened and a middle aged woman in the doorway facing the man who must be Smith-Heritage, the man whom Lynch had seen that morning quartering Runneymede. She was wearing a nondescript raincoat and a faded headscarf. The man spoke to her briefly and handed her an envelope. She took it and left, disappearing out of Lynch's sight. Smith-Heritage stood in the doorway for a moment, watching, then went back inside and closed the door. The woman reappeared in Lynch's sight again passing further down the drive, pushing a bicycle. The daily woman, probably. But did she minister to Number 32 every day or on two or three days a week? It might be useful to know; it might not be useful at all, but he could do with a change of activity. He thought that so long as the car remained at the front door there wasn't much he could do anyway. He went back to his own car.

The lady on the bicycle had not passed him so she must have turned right at the gate. He made a quiet, careful three point turn and took the same route, catching sight of her in a few seconds. He followed slowly and discreetly.

At the main road she dismounted, wheeled her bicycle across to the other side, remounted and rode off again, right, then turned left into a congeries of small terraced houses. When she stopped at a brightly painted house with white palings, Lynch drove past, and saw her wheel the bicycle up the concrete path and round to the back. He stopped half a dozen houses beyond.

The house he chose, after careful inspection, had old fashioned window blinds with white tassels which he had not seen for a generation. He raised the gleaming brass horseshoe and knocked firmly. Somewhere in the rear a terrier erupted in yelping fury. He heard an interior door shut and the barking suddenly diminuendo. The front door opened and he was confronted, as he had anticipated he might be, by an elderly woman — late seventies, perhaps. Her hair was white and she peered at him through thick spectacles that might signal cataract. She wore a clean flowered pinafore and leaned on a stout ash cane.

'Good evening,' said Lynch, 'I wonder whether I've come to the right place. I'm looking for someone to give my wife a hand with the housework and I was given this address — '

The old girl was laughing heartily. 'No good looking at me, son, I could do with someone to give me a hand, don't you think? No it's Number 8 down the road you want. She does for people, I think; I don't know her, mind you, for she's new here and I don't get out much, but, from what I hear, she's the one you want.'

'That's Mrs Phillips is it?'

'No, not Phillips, Townsend, Mrs Townsend. You try there.'

Lynch thanked her and went back to his car; her sight wasn't very good, he doubted whether she could describe him. He hoped that nobody would ever ask her for a description.

He drove back down on to the main road.

The telephone box was empty — and unvandalized — juvenile delinquency shrinking under the sheer weight of Sunningdale opulence — or perhaps all the kids were at boarding school, and kicking hell out of Harrow. There was also, miracle of miracles, a local directory — intact. One could easily get to like Sunningdale.

His guess was right, if not particularly brilliant: charladies these days needed telephones and transport to stay in business.

She answered quickly, 'This is Mrs Townsend, who's calling?'

'We need a bit of help in the house,' lied Lynch, glibly, in his best Home Counties accent, 'and we wondered whether you had a morning or an afternoon to spare.'

'I'm sorry. I'm full right up, just couldn't fit another soul in.'

'We live up in Blythswood Drive and you do go up there, don't you?'

'That's right. Mr Smith-Heritage.'

'Mr' not 'Mrs' Lynch noted.

'I thought, since you were in the Drive, anyway, you might be able to give us a couple of hours.'

'No. I'm sorry. I do Mr Smith-Heritage Wednesday afternoon and Saturday afternoon, and I'm there right up till tea time, just couldn't squeeze in anybody else. Sorry. I do have a waiting list of ladies, as well. Goodbye.'

Lynch could understand her abrupt ringing off: he could do with his tea too. He wished he had a waiting list of ladies.

The hegira from the City was in full cry, the Executive stampeding to the lush watering holes of Surrey and Berkshire in a continuous belt of metal and rubber. Only when a sudden emptiness betokened the closure of the level crossing gates was he able to make a right turn back on to the A30.

Driving up Blythswood Drive for the second time he met a police panda cruising down, unhurried, attendant on the lodges of the well breeched lieges. At the crook of the crescent he drove up on to the clipped grass verge, stopped, got out, lifted up the bonnet. When you waited for the AA to come to your assistance you lifted up the bonnet so that the breakdown wagon would recognise you: everybody knew that, took it for granted, ceased to be curious; he hoped.

He got back in to the driving seat, munched a few biscuits, drank some coffee from the flask, and kept one ear cocked for the distinctive sound of an Aston Martin growling into life. Occasionally, a homeward bound car passed him, the driver averting his eyes quickly from the upraised bonnet lest he be importuned for a spanner, or the use of a telephone, or a word of sympathy.

From time to time he got out and paced up and down between the car and his 'leper squint' at Number 32, modelling the impatient sentry beat of the stranded motorist everywhere. Of course the AA people were efficient, but in the Summer they got a lot of calls, so you paced up and down: everybody knew that, took it for granted, ceased to be curious. There was nobody around to be curious. Nothing happened until nearly nine o'clock, when just as he was turning away from Number 32 for the umpteenth time, the front door opened and Smith-Heritage came out, alone, and closed the door behind him. He was dressed in a fawn, lightweight, linen suit, a lemon silk shirt, a different cravat this time, midnight blue. He opened a gold cigar case just before he slid into the driver's seat, looked carefully at the contents, then slipped it back into his inside jacket pocket. A gentleman out for the evening. With Ramsden perhaps? A Ramsden kept discreetly, but necessarily, just out of ambit; to be met offstage, only when necessary.

Lynch took off at a tiptoe-ing run. If Smith-Heritage turned left, out of his driveway, then Lynch was in trouble; the C.O. would be alive to the slightest disharmony — like a pedestrian — like Lynch — like a broken down car not a hundred miles from his house.

He reached Number 34, concealed by the curvature of the Drive from the gates of Number 32, but only just — the engine note swelled, held steady, then faded — the Aston Martin had gone right. He slowed down to a walk, and when he reached his own car, he put the bonnet down, got in and made his own way, slowly, back down to the main road.

The unblemished telephone box was empty again; perhaps it was only there for the passing poor. He rang the Smith-Heritage number; nobody answered; he let the bell ring for five minutes before he put the phone down. No wife then, no stay at home Cinders of a Ramsden, no anybody.

He returned to his previous parking place, walked back, and turned unhesitatingly into the drive of Number 32. The herbaceous borders, he noticed were completely free of weeds, the standard roses as uniform as a guard of honour — it looked as if the Colonel might have a gardener as well as a charlady. The immediate question was whether he had a dog or not.

He rang the door bell boldly; he could always say he was a canvasser for the local Liberal Party, or the Total Abstainers

League, or something. Nothing happened; he waited; rang again; still silence. No dog then.

The windows at the front were all secure; high up on the right, under the eaves, a red box jutted out, wires spidering to right and to left. A burglar conscious householder this one. The matching double garage was fast locked; through a window Lynch could see an aluminium extending ladder hung on a wall, a wide waist-high work bench, well stocked with vices; clamps, power tools, a welder's visor. A man of parts, the Colonel. But no second car for the lady of the house to go a-marketing. So, no Colonel's lady?

Behind the house a stone flagged terrace lipped a shimmering blue tiled swimming pool; a fitted carpet of green lawn sported gleaming, white, wrought iron garden furniture, a central pedestalled sundial; and washed up against a feathery backdrop of darkening fir. A proud and private demesne the brave Colonel had and the wherewithal to keep it so, it seemed. And all stapled up tight as a bank? Perhaps.

The daylight was thinning, the stuffing gone out of it as Lynch moved quietly out and back to his car. The tall graceful lamp standards glowed into unobtrusive lambency, brushing high branches pale yellow, as he drove away. He wondered where Ramsden was stashed. Not near Staines or Kingston, that was for sure, but near enough for stand-to and C.O.'s 'orders'. Friday had to be a two man operation, like Brace and Clelland, or Valerie Scott. But was Valerie Scott their operation at all? Or was he forcing the unfitting pieces into the jigsaw because he wanted to, didn't know what else to do. Maybe he would find out.

Back at the 'Crusader' people sat about in the gardens, long drinks in their clasped hands, relaxing, savouring the blue twilight. In the bar there was an undertone of Arpege sweetening the aroma of priceless Havana, the body odour of the arrivées.

He swallowed a double Glenlivet too quickly for justice and went to his room. There was a pile of sandwiches, covered over with a damp square of towel, three bottles of cold Guinness, an opener and a thick pewter tankard. Biddy never forgot. He dialled Frances's number at Datchet before doing anything else but there was no reply; he didn't seem to be having a lot of success with the telephone these days; he wished he had kept his semaphore up to scratch. Perhaps she was at P.T.A. meeting, or a staff outing to the theatre, or she had found another feller. Maybe she was just bored with the whole concept of Patrick Lynch and wasn't answering the telephone; he wouldn't blame her; he was a little bored with the concept himself.

He uncovered the sandwiches, filled the tankard till it spilled over, and fell to. Through the open window came peals of happy laughter in the gloaming, the tinkle of glasses, the persistent bass thrumming of inconsequential talk, a symphony for a summer evening.

He threw himself on the bed and opened his battered copy of Lamb's

Essays at random, to escape into the sadly serene world of the gentle Elia. He never got his girl either, he reflected, but then not many of us do.

16

He rang before breakfast, and this time she answered.

'Pat! Where have you been? I've been worried.'

'Chasing will o' the wisps, not getting very far. I rang last night — '

'Oh, hell! We had a Maths consortium last night. No. It isn't. It's quite proper actually. Except that this one dragged on till eleven o'clock. Never mind; what about today? Damn! I'm on duty at lunch time for half an hour.'

'Tonight, Frances?'

'Oh, yes. Tell you what: dinner at my place. Goulash and bucketsful of Lager. You fancy?'

'I fancy. Heavy on the paprika; plenty of ice for the beer.'

'Yes, master; no, master. There is a very old Chinese proverb which I have this minute invented which says 'He who orders the cook around in her kitchen lies down with empty belly.' You savee?'

'There is nothing that delights a man in a woman more than submissiveness. I savee. What time?'

'Shall we say seven thirty for eight. My goulash will not be hurried. I must fly or I'll be late for work. And I have not been setting such a good example these days, according to the Head of Scriptures — she saw us in Datchet on Saturday. Quite overcome she was, poor dear. Goodbye.'

Lynch hung up with a sense of loss. Frances was a woman a man could cling to.

He spent the early part of the morning shopping around in Staines for the things he needed, or might need, on the morrow; he bought the most incriminating items separately so as not to fix himself in anybody's mind. The man in the ironmonger's looked at him quizzically, however, when he bought the elbow length jemmy, 'Something to stir your porridge with, eh? I know: none of my business, but if the old Bill catches you with that on you, have to have a very good explanation.'

'Not to worry,' cried Lynch as he left the shop, 'it's for my night school course — City and Guilds — Advanced Breaking and Entering. If you fail they sentence you to go straight.'

By half past eleven he had bought all the things he knew he would need, and all the things he could think of that he might need. He took them back to the 'Crusader', keeping strictly to the speed limits all the way; one peep into the stained, canvas toolbag he had bought, second hand, to hold his purchases and even the laziest traffic policeman would have escorted him back to the station. And how would one explain them, separately or collectively. He could hear the interrogation in his head.

'And the tinman's snips, sir?

'Oh, you're a sculptor, creating dynamic, free standing, non-functional forms out of the discards and the detritus of a mechanical and mechanistic society. And that explains the hacksaw, too? Of course it does.

'What about the glass cutters, sir?

‘But I do understand the challenge of industrial jetsam, I assure you, sir; we all do at this station.

‘And the NEW jemmy? and the NEW rubber suction pad?

‘For your new masterpiece the ‘Defloration of Ceres’? Very symbolical, too, if you don’t mind my saying so.

‘But what an aesthetic gent like yourself wouldn’t realise is that all your sculptor’s implements can be put to illicit use. Word of honour, sir. ‘Going equipped’ we call it in the trade. So we’ll just nip round to your studio —

‘You haven’t got a studio, yet, just the tools? Oh, don’t worry about it. My inspector will understand when you tell him.

‘Oh, no, sir. Nothing Philistine about him. Great one for the art he is. First thing he does when he opens the paper is turn to the cartoons, then the pictures. Sometimes never reads a word of print, just the cartoons and the pictures. He’s an artistic wee bobby is our inspector.’

So, it behoved him to drive with lawful primness back to the ‘Crusader’ and not expose himself to the shrewd irony of an inquisitive police force. He did, a 'verray parfait gentil knyght' of the dual carriageway, and reached sanctuary safely.

Up in his room, he sorted quickly through his purchases of the morning, added the still unloaded gun, and the cartridges, and locked the bulging toolbag in the cavernous teak wardrobe which must have been a bus garage in a previous incarnation. Then he went, restlessly, downstairs.

The pre-prandial stampede in the bar reminded him of Cup Final day at Wembley Stadium, so he gave it a miss, and went outside to sit uneasily in a deck chair and suck at an acrid, empty pipe. He felt as he used to do during the long wait in the assembly area, before you moved up to the start line and zero hour, and, finally, action, the explosive relief from suspense. You played cards wthout zeal, made forcedly flippant remarks, got up, sat down, queued up at the latrine for the fifth time, and checked your rifle for the twentieth time. Any activity to banish fearful anticipation, to blunt the tedium of snail ticking time.

Sucking an empty pipe for the next eight hours was hardly the solution.

He went to his car.

A green van was parked inside the entrance to Number 32 Blythswood Drive, Sunningdale, when Lynch cruised past at twelve fifteen. He read the blazon on the back doors as he changed down: 'Jaconelli Brothers, Contract Gardeners.' Two dark haired young men moved along the herbaceous border, the sun glinting off their bare, sweaty, olive torsos. There was no sign of the Aston Martin or Ramsden's Jaguar. Perhaps the two of them were out, 'tooling up' for the next day, just as he had been doing. Maybe not. What was it W. S. Gilbert had said about the felon and 'his capacity for innocent enjoyment'? They could be out paying the rates, chatting up a barmaid over a pub lunch, 'mugging' old ladies, 'Paki-bashing', kidnapping guide dogs — the everyday social round. Whatever they were doing, they didn't need Lynch to help them do it. He left.

Back on the A30 he turned off at

Virginia Water, drove South through Byfleet, bore East and South, twisting and turning until he reached Box Hill. The Ordnance Survey Map said 541 feet to Juniper Top, so it wasn't K2; it wasn't even Snowdon or Ben Macdhuie but it would be enough to take the edge off his jumpiness: physical expenditure usually did, and in his condition, Box Hill would be more than a match for his damned up tension.

The car park below the hill was a side pocket off the A24 into Dorking, nearly empty, when he drove in and parked. As he got out, a coach drew away, bearing, according to the legend on the side, a passenger load of disabled ex-service men. Lynch stole a quick glance in as it moved past him — a container of hoary headed, quiet, elderly men. Why did such a congregation always embarrass and shame a little? Perhaps because Crete, and El Alamein, and Monte Cassino had left them living but sheared the use out of their young lives so that they drew out the rest of their days, not as plumbers or brickies or tycoons, or harassed fathers, but as battle casualties, paying by daily instalments unto death the high price of our freedom and wholeness.

He tried to shrug off the momentary futile sadness: maybe they didn't see it like that; he hoped not.

On the left of the hotel buildings a chalk scar laddered whitely up, lancing the green hill — the direct line. He took it, brave for the first forty yards, then labouring and blowing, stopping and straining for breath every few minutes until he gained the gentle slope running up to the top plateau and sat down hastily. K2, and Snowdon, and Ben Macdhuie could rest easy for a while: he wasn't ready for them yet.

A glance at his watch drove him down again for a quick light lunch: salad and coffee, though he panted after beer. Then up again, teeth gritting, chest heaving until he had reconquered it as he had foolishly promised himself.

After another rest he walked on slowly until he entered the lofty hall of trees that cowled the crest. He had determined to go as far as the mad Major, if the Mad

Major was still in situ. He was.

The simple headstone stood relatively unscathed on its low white plinth:

'Major Peter Labelliere
Aged 75
An eccentric resident of Dorking
was buried here, head downwards
11 July 1800'

Lynch looked around: a peristyle of tall, fragrant trees, bosky English Gothic pierced by shafts of diffused light, an organ loft of birdsong, just in earshot. Was he so eccentric, the Mad Major, with his cool shadowy cathedral all to himself? He turned back, and came out into the sun again, blinking, detouring round a young teacher seated on the ground, her ten-year-olds strewn around her like confetti. She was reading aloud to them as he passed and he caught a teasing fragment: 'He died at the age of ninety-five, and in his will he directed that his children should dance . . . ' Dance a what? Dance where? Lynch carried on, never to know. And he was the one who said to

Price-Carruthers that he wasn't 'a collector of testamentary bric-a-brac'. And from Richard Scott to the Mad Major to this young woman's never to be recaptured nonagenarian he was being tagged by whimsical will-makers!

A little way down the hill he eased himself down on the cropped turf and treated himself to a pipe as he scanned the map and tried to pinpoint the evocative labels on the ground before him: Juniper Hall, Druid's Grove, Badger's Farm, Crabtree Cottage, Polesden Lacey, Camilla Lacey — a very Debrett of English place names. But his map reading skill seemed to have rusted thin in recent years; you didn't need a cartographer for slopping out in one of Her Majesty's nicks; and such was the palisading of evergreens that all the myth charged names remained just printed symbols with no substance. Only a hand of stiff fingered Tudor chimneys thrusting out of the treetops which might have been the tuft on the head of Juniper Hall. Or it might not.

He folded the map up, tapped his pipe

out, and lay recumbent on the grass with his eyes closed. He couldn't think of anything to do but let the day slither on at its own pace.

When he woke up it was nearly six, and the last washes of prison pallor were burning out of his face. A small, hard, multicoloured ball lay on his stomach, and a Jack Russell terrier hovered over him, expectantly. There was no sign of an owner.

'It's a very silly and dangerous thing to do, dog,' he said, 'picking up stray people — you never know where they've been.'

He got to his feet stiffly, and threw the ball hard down the eastern slope. As the white blur dropped out of sight below, Lynch took off in the opposite direction, down to Burford Bridge and the car park.

By seven he had showered and changed into fresh clothes and was trying to placate an irate Biddy, which was like saying 'shush' to a battery of heavy artillery.

'They'll be taking us out of the Good Food Guide if you carry on like this. You don't have to tell me we're not in the

Good Food Guide; I know that as well as you; we don't want to be in it; we included ourselves out as a matter of policy if you must know. Oh, you do know. But if it was left to people like you always turning up their noses at my cooking we'd never get into it at all.'

Tactfully he attempted to stem the flow.

'Then why don't you bring her here for dinner? Afraid somebody'll ask you if your granddaughter's enjoying her meal?'

He tried to show how it wasn't like that.

Biddy sighed. 'Why do they do it? Skip lunch, rush round the shops buying cuts of meat they can't really afford, race home in the evening, spend hours over the stove, five minutes to make their face up and splash on some cologne. And for what? Some randy old lecher like you with a bottle of cheap plonk and a trough full of aftershave over him wondering which he should rush for first — the table or the bed! Is she a good cook?'

Lynch kissed his finger tips, 'Cordon Bleu! In another twenty years she'll be in your class.'

She walloped him on the rump, 'Bloody Clydeside Casanova! And remember this: you'll be able to enjoy a good meal when you're too old to enjoy other things. Off you go.'

As he made his way to Datchet through the thinning traffic he gave his mind over to the philosophy and ethic of lying. At ordinary everyday, commercial, white lying, long practice and experience had put him in the master class. He had discovered, early in life, that, where truth was unprofitable, he could, almost always, tailor a falsehood, snug enough and plausible enough to attain his end. Means and ends; that's what it was about; and people. Even yet he doubted whether he could ever lie to a Catholic priest, however praiseworthy the motive. One up for school confessions and the penny catechism. Nor had he ever been able to lie to absolve himself of personal guilt or responsibility. He could still see his C.O.'s angry face when he was awarded his first 'jankers'.

'Not the whole truth, sir. I told the guard commander he could shove his bayonet frog up as well.'

And what end had that prideful little nugget attained? An extra seven days C.B. that he needn't have had and didn't enjoy.

However, when you wanted an address from a suspicious relative you were more likely to get it by saying you wanted to give the errant husband a sweepstake prize, than by telling the truth about his deserted wife waiting vainly for her overdue alimony.

So you bore false witness, oiling the bearings of the task, and increasing the chances of achieving what you were being paid to achieve. And it was impersonal, did no harm to the godly, and, with luck, smote the evildoer in the nuts. But to deceive your own, to lie to people you respected, loved even! That was a horse of a very different colour. His stomach churned. How on earth was he going to manage it with Frances Gavin, of the transparently honest face and the trusting mind, who would accept anything he said as if it were graven on a stone tablet? He supposed the end was right, though the means would bring bile to his throat. He lifted his foot off the accelerator and slowed down. He could turn round and go back and do it by phone, a less honest dishonesty; and he wouldn't have to look into her eyes afterwards and eat her food, and brush her off in her own house.

He pressed his foot down again; it had to work; and the only way to give the lie a chance of success was the hard way. The hard way it had to be.

17

Frances greeted him in the open doorway, held him tight.

'I was hoping you'd be early.'

'Sorry. I didn't want the goulash to feel it was being chivvied.'

She was wearing a simple summer frock, the same fierce blue as her eyes; her long shapely legs were bare to matching espadrilles; there were tiny beads of sweat on her brow, a heightened rosiness in her cheeks.

'You smell like an old fashioned farmhouse kitchen, warm, spicy, mouth wateringly edible.'

''Shall I compare thee to a baker's oven?' You've a way with a compliment that could get your eye blacked. Did you know that? Nice to see you, Lynch. You can let me go in a minute, but not yet.'

'What about the Head of Scripture?'

'Pish! A murrain on her, and on her ox and on her ass unto the umpteenth generation. So there!'

She released him with a sigh of regret, 'That'll have to do for now, I suppose. Come into the kitchen. I have a neurotic cooker so I brought the drinks in here where I can watch over it. It's a manic depressive, really, and I've had to keep it very low, very melancholy all evening. It's liable to go berserk any minute now.'

Lynch went back out and brought in his presents from the car, the two bottles, the tissue wrapped carving.

'Goody! Presents! I should be remembering that hackneyed old tag from Virgil. What is it 'Timeo Danaos — ''

'' — et dona ferentes.'' finished Lynch, 'This timid old Greek you need not fear, nor his piddling little gifts — a bottle of port to reflect on the glory of your goulash, a bottle of Drambuie to replenish your father's plundered stock, and a gewgaw for yourself, woman of the house.'

She unwrapped the tissue and held the kneeling fawn in her palm, caressed the delicate back with a wondering finger.

'Lovely present. Lovely man. Bless you,

Pat! I'll put it on my desk. It will refresh me to look at it when the marking becomes too much for me, which is usually after about five minutes.'

'There's a woodcarver in Knutsford. It was on my way.'

She left the kitchen, calling over her shoulder as she went, 'Drinks on the dresser, Cinzano for me, giant family size, with plenty of ice. And there's a fresh bottle of whisky — from the Orkneys — my grocer wished it on me, said it was good.'

Lynch eyed the bottle, 'He did not lie; genuine twenty four carat water of life. Cleave to your grocer.'

'You'd better enjoy it,' she urged, as she returned 'I'm not going to be able to buy tights for a year.'

He busied himself with bottles and glasses while Frances fretted at the stove.

'Well! What happened?'

He kept his back to her, being clumsy with the ice tray. It was easier not to face her.

'Dead end. Ramsden is not Cooper. It was a good hypothesis while it lasted.'

He handed her her drink, his eyes fixed on the brimming-over liquid, evading hers.

'Too much ice.'

He went back to the dresser, telling himself that it was for her own good, but that did not improve anything.

'You found Ramsden then?'

He fumbled with the whisky bottle.

'Not exactly. But I found the girls he left behind him, so to speak; it took time. About a year after his run in with Valerie he gave up the racing game, or it gave him up; anyway he took the Queen's shilling and joined the Colours. He's in Germany right now so I didn't speak with him. But I checked; there's no way Sergeant Ramsden could have spent a year cleaning windows.'

There! It was done. He turned towards her.

'You did your best, Pat. Come on, let's eat.'

They ate in the kitchen, drank Arctic lager, and talked inconsequentially.

'Coffee in the sitting room. The washing up will keep until tomorrow.'

He carried in the bottles, poured two glasses of port and sat down in the deep easy chair, 'You wield a mean skillet, lady, a man could get fat and contented round you.'

She laughed, 'That's the mesage I've been trying to get across. Communication has been established.'

She brought the tray in, put it down, and went over to the record player.

'I know this record's been played to death but it seems suitable now.'

They sipped their coffee and drank their port and lost themselves in the 'Concierto de Aranjuez', the guitar swelling, dying, hushing, holding.

'For Valerie?' he asked, as the last chord faded in the sun swept room.

She nodded.

'Like that piece,' he mused aloud, 'what's it called now? I know: 'Pavane for a Dead Infanta', something like that.'

'In a way; only this is more — well it's just more.'

Lynch lit his pipe and let the sad silence lengthen.

'You know, Pat,' she began tentatively.

'You puzzle me. All these contradictions. You're perceptive, no, sensitive, and compassionate; at least I feel you to be so; you're on my wave length; and yet — '

'And yet?'

'You pleaded guilty to beating a man near to death.'

'Strapper? Oh, well, we're all of us Jekyll and Hyde, yin and yang, saint and sinner. I'm no different.'

'Yes, but to beat someone like that. There I can't empathize, if that's the word. Tell me about it. Tell me about Strapper. I want to know; I want to know about you.'

'I'll tell you, since you ask, but there isn't much.'

He got up and refilled the coffee cups. She took hers, mechanically, her eyes grave now, intent on his.

'Some two years ago a middle aged woman engaged me to find her daughter. Mrs Cordell. She was a widow, kept a shop in a village in Staffordshire. She had one daughter just turned seventeen, who, like thousands of others, had fled home and hearth for the bright lights of

London. Unlike the other thousands, however, this girl, Tina, was mentally retarded. That's not how Mrs Cordell would put it: 'a bit backward' was as far as she would go, but that was a mum speaking. Anyway, I found Tina in Strapper's stable — '

'Stable? She was looking after — '

'No Frances, she wasn't grooming horses, or cleaning tack. Strapper runs a club in Soho but his main income comes from a small, carefully chosen string of prostitutes — all young, all pretty, all high earners.'

'Pat, these words, 'string', and 'stable': they're obscene.'

'Strapper's words; he likes using them, but then he is an obscenity himself.'

'But you said this girl, Tina, was sub-normal — aren't there laws?'

'She had not been classified as a mental defective, though she had been to a school for the educationally sub-normal. I think she could have been classified but she wasn't. I suppose, in a way, her appearance was against her: physically, she was completely normal: too much so, in fact; sexually ripening, the way Strapper likes his so called hostesses — '

'Foul!'

'It's a foul world, in parts, my love. I found the flat where Strapper had installed her. I took her mother there, in the hope that when she was actually confronted with her mother she might have been coaxed back home. We might have pulled it off, too.'

'Might have?'

'Unfortunately, Strapper was with her. 'Looking after her interests,' he said. My mistake. I should have ensured that he wouldn't be there; I didn't so I failed Mrs Cordell — and Tina. It was, as they say, a bad scene. She screamed abuse at her mother, used words a seventeen year old should never even have heard, clung to Strapper, swore she was going to marry him — probably believed it, too.'

'What did you do?'

'Nothing I could do. There's no way of forcing a seventeen year old girl back home, if she doesn't want to go, as Strapper knew. Eventually, Mrs Cordell could take no more and ran out of the flat. I went after her, calmed her down as best as I could, and put her on a train back to Staffordshire.'

'But the police — '

'They do their best, but Strapper's girls bring him enough money to buy the best legal advice in King's Bench Walk, if he needs it.'

'So that's why — '

'I don't like to see a mum being stamped into the dirt by the Strappers of the world, nor children debauched by them. I went to Strapper's club late that night, bluffed my way past his 'minders' and caught him in his office, alone. He was counting the takings from the night. I locked the door and stamped him into the dirt. I didn't put him out of business; he still runs his stable, but he has to take a painkiller now and again.'

'And Tina?'

'I've only been out a few weeks, remember. I don't know. Still working for Strapper or somebody like him, I expect. You don't see many happy endings nowadays.'

Frances shivered.

‘Was it worth two years in jail?’

‘Equations, sequations! I could never make head nor tail of them. I can’t look at things that way. That’s the tale of Strapper and me. I told you it wasn’t much.’

‘I can see that there was a certain kind of justice or retribution in what you did, but I can’t see myself able to take the law into my own hands like that.’

Lynch stood up, ruffled, in spite of himself, and poured himself a drink.

‘Fine. Don’t, if you cannot. But you’re a bright, well-educated, liberated, twentieth century miss, so don’t let yourself be duped by the self serving propaganda of our own employees. It is your law, my law, which we empower and pay the courts and the police to impose for all of us. They believe, and would have you believe, that to take our own law back into our own hands, no matter how good the reason, is almost as heinous as treason. True, it is usually untidy, and sometimes inaccurate and inefficient, but it is not the moral outrage that we are conditioned to see it is.’

'You're not conditioned, though?'

'Let us say I deconditioned myself a long time ago. I think the 'leave it to the copper on the beat' philosophy has had a debilitating effect on us. If the dear old neighbourhood bobby cannot or will not deal with a wrong we are incapable, now, of righting it ourselves. We've been psyched out of doing it for hundreds of years.'

'But where there is no law broken as in Tina's case?'

'Should we pass a law to protect the Tinas from the Strappers?'

'Of course. I'm sure most people would think so.'

'So, maybe in five or six years' time we'll get such a law on the statute book. But meanwhile there are Tinas abroad — and Strappers to do them dirty if we let them.'

'And you won't let them?'

'Look, I'm no Don Quixote, or Robin Hood; I'm certainly not Edgar Wallace's Fifth Just Man. This is largely a personal thing; if someone does me, or mine, wrong, and my law and my law enforcers fail me, then I won't shrink from exacting my own satisfaction, or vengeance, if you like. But there's no danger of me taking business away from the Ombudsman, or the Citizen's Advice Bureau.'

'Lynch's Law — an eye for an eye, straight back to the Old Testament.'

'Back beyond the Old Testament, beyond Hammurabi, back into the caves primeval, if you worry about provenance.'

'But Tina wasn't one of yours, was she? It wasn't personal.'

'No, and yes. It wasn't personal, but I had taken Mrs Cordell's money — it was a kind of adoption, I suppose; it felt personal.'

'And if Ramsden HAD been Cooper would you have adopted Valerie? Would it have felt personal?'

Lynch shuffled his feet and decided to sit down; her probes were touching raw nerves now.

'If Ramsden HAD been Cooper he could have been ticketed for Brace and Clelland, he could have been linked to Valerie; the law keepers would have had a chance.'

‘So Cooper robbed Brace and Clelland but did not kill Val.’

‘Not necessarily; Cooper, wherever he is could still be linked to Valerie in a way that nobody will ever find out unless Cooper were to tell.’

‘Pat, I’m glad Ramsden wasn’t Cooper. I hope, now, that you don’t find Cooper. Because, if you do, you might apply Lynch’s Law to him. And I don’t like that, I can’t convince myself it’s right.’

‘How could you? When we start to pay a hangman we distance ourselves from the act, and we’ve been paying our executioners for a long time now. So, when there is no hangman, we let the murderer live, with many rationalizations and justifications. Fine. But let us also recognise that we have simply lost the stomach for doing the unpleasant, or the brutal, even when it is right to do them.’

‘True of me, certainly, Pat. I’ve always been kept removed from gallows, and slaughter houses and sewage works, barricaded in my nice comfortable existence against the harsh realities of living and dying. I can’t help it, and I don't think I can change, I'm sorry.'

'Don't be sorry. You're a delightful, honest you. No one would want you changed; I know I wouldn't.'

'I'm glad you think so, Pat Lynch. So what are you going to do about it?'

'You mean right this minute?'

'No. Yes. Oh, you know what I mean.'

'I do, so help me, and I'm going to try my damnedest not to do anything about it.'

Her lip trembled and she gnawed at it.

'I wish I could be all ladylike about this but I can't so I'm going to ask you why not, if I may.'

He fought hard not to take her hands in his.

'And I'll try to tell you, my dear, dear Frances. For one thing, I'm a generation older than you. For another, I like moving around, drinking, gambling, the sharp edge of reality. I even enjoy violence, to be honest, though not so much now perhaps, as I once did. I know what I am, an ageing fly man from Govan with a high I.Q. and a superficial gloss, handy with a headbutt or an aphorism. Here today and gone today, a fugitive from the steady job and the hard, lifelong, slog. A long term prospect I am not.'

Her voice was firmer now.

'So, you are here today, and not gone yet. No one said anything about long term agreements.'

'Wrong. I did. Because that's what you're worth. And you're not to be codded out of it — not by me — not by yourself either, come to that.'

'You never codded me.'

'Didn't I? I wouldn't like to take a bible oath on it. You will settle for some lucky, lucky man of your time, your own ambience, who'll wed you, and bed you, and bairn you; who'll work his skull off for you for the rest of his days and feel privileged to do so. You will not settle for less, for less is not worthy of you.'

She looked across at him, her eyes glinting.

'Pat Lynch, I wasn't trying to take out a 99 year lease on you.'

He went over to her where she sat, touched her hair.

'You could have it freehold, my love, but the property isn't worth a damn, I know.'

She caught his hand, held it for a moment.

'My survey said it was fine.'

He disengaged his hand, gently, and went over to the open window: a flotilla of ducks charged across the water to where a small boy waited with a paper bag; a black Labrador climbed out and shook himself vigorously over a couple couchant on the bank; an ice cream van trundled past, solitary, unhurried; the sun varnished the still leaves of the trees across the river.

'I think,' came her voice behind him, 'it's time for lightweight music and non-committal conversation, the 'shoes and ships and sealing wax' hour.'

She was kneeling on the carpet picking through records.

He returned to his seat.

She arranged a little pile, and slipped them on to the record player, 'A rung above Muzak, but nothing more mind blowing than Simon, or Loussier.' She sat back in her chair and regarded him mischievously 'Pretend you've just picked me up, Lynch, and make with the persiflage; you know the sort of thing, inspired attention getters that sweep a girl off her feet like 'Do you come here often?' '

'Or, 'When's the last bus back frae your house?' ' countered Lynch, swiftly. 'That was always my opening gambit on the palais floor.'

'Sheer poetry — epic! I bet that made many a shy maid swoon.'

'Every sequin quivered — separately. Also it prevented me embarking on campaigns that geography and tight timetables would have rendered fruitless. I learned the hard way. Do you know I once bought a girl three cokes and a hot mutton pie, all in the same evening, mark you, and I didn't learn until the last waltz that she lived in Auchenshuggle. Auchenshuggle! They send St Bernards out after you there.'

Frances giggled, 'Auchenshuggle! There's no such place.'

'I've always had doubts, myself, and

that girl was the only person I ever met in my life who actually admitted to living there. But it must exist, Frances, I've seen the name on the bus destination boards; Glasgow Corporation wouldn't lie about a thing like that — unless — '

So they pulled the evening slowly and happily through their fingers, with aimless chatter, and close companionable silences, and the smooth lubricant of comforting music.

When it grew too dark to see her he got up, switched on a single floor lamp and sat back, taking her in all over again, etching into his memory plates the clear, bold line of the jaw, the glow of her skin, the tidal lustre of the dark hair, the arched, black brows.

She turned the records over and still they talked as the night tip-toed on. Eventually, he stole a reluctant look at his watch.

'Quarter to midnight. Time I was away.'

'I suppose so, Pat,' she sighed. 'But away to what? What will you do now? Not about us; you're not going to do anything about us, for your own good reasons, though they may not be as good as you think. But about you? There doesn't seem to be anything more you can do about Val, does there?'

'Not unless you can come up with something or somebody, or the police come up with something new, and that doesn't look very likely. No. Tomorrow, I think I'll drive to Dover, take the ferry, motor straight down to Marseille and turn left for the Cote d'Azur.'

'You wouldn't take a girl along for the ride?'

'To Saint Tropez? Carry coals to Newcastle?' His smile robbed the remark of its sting. 'I'll swim, lie in the sun, play the tables, paddle my own pedalo, and, as my old man used to say 'Curse the Irish, for the Scots are cursed already'. And when I've had enough I'll come back and start my private peeking all over again.'

'The sharp edge of reality? Whatever happens to private detectives when they grow old? Do they have a pension scheme or an old detectives' home?'

'They grow smaller and smaller until

they finally disappear up a keyhole, clutching a padded expense account, and they're never seen again.'

He made his way along the narrow hallway, and she came with him, her arm around him, her hair brushing his cheek.

'It's been nice knowing you, Patrick Aloysius Cameron Lynch. Come again. Anytime. You don't have to wait until there's a murder, or a race riot, or an uprising against the Civil Power.'

'Send me an invitation care of the 'Crusader' and I'll come to your wedding.'

'Wedding! With men like you about I could finish up the youngest old maid in Datchet, if you know what I mean.'

He got into his car, started up, switched on the lights against the dark. She bent over him and kissed him fiercely on the mouth, 'Sometimes short term leases are good too.'

He backed on to the road in a snarling agony of rubber, fluttered a hand in farewell, and launched the car at the bend, foot down. He thought that if he were to stop at the first suitably virgin wall and paint 'Chastity rules. OK?' with his purple aerosol spray he might feel better. Only he didn't have a purple aerosol spray, and nobody would believe him, anyway: it was a bloody silly slogan.

18

The G.P.O. alarm call he had placed the night before slapped him awake, mercilessly, at half past five on Friday morning. He showered and shaved, donned lightweight slacks and thin T-shirt, then drew on the blotched one-piece overalls he had bought second, or twenty-second, hand in Staines the previous day. Even after the pricey ministrations of the 'Lightning One Hour Dry Cleaners' he could still detect malodorous traces of a long line of previous occupants. But, since they were the only overalls he had, he buttoned them up and thought, bravely, of England. His decrepit chukka boots were disreputable enough to blend with the overalls, but were still snug and pliant on his feet, and noiseless.

Through his windows the light eased in, pearly and faintly iridescent, with the promise of another peerless day. The 'Crusader' slumbered on, the snorings and tossings of its lodgers crumbling against the thick old walls of its bedchambers, bottled and impotent. The birds were piping their limited lien of the unpolluted morning.

Without the aid of a compass, he rescued the heavy toolbag from the unchartered recesses of the vast wardrobe. Then he pulled the woolly pompom bonnet over his head and looked in the mirror: 'the glass of fashion and the mould of form', everywoman's idea of her friendly neighbourhood plumber — or gasfitter — or glazier, agog for his first tea-break. He was ready. Closing the door, he went softly down the wide rheumaticky staircase and out into the burgeoning day.

His car was parked well down the drive to minimise the chances of his early departure wafting through the open window of a nosy insomniac with a photographic memory and a great nephew in the Metropolitan Police. He walked on the grass until he was out of range of the house, his soundless steps printing a faint white spoor on the green fur. A rabbit at early breakfast looked up, startled, and scuttled off to another eating house. It had Lynch's sympathy: he, too, liked his petit dejeuner undisturbed.

The engine fired immediately, gagging the birds, breaching the unpeopled serenity of the vista-spoked gardens, raping the still air. He pushed in the choke, reined the engine down to a half heard throb and sailed, silkily down on to the empty road, unreeling like a taut white ribbon before him.

It was getting on for half past six when he gained Sunningdale Station. Already the car park was colour patched with early cars, their drivers measuring the platform like solitary drill sergeants. A vegetable lorry trundled heavily over the railway lines; a solitary cyclist, head retracted tortoise-like, bucked across purposefully.

Lynch parked near the entrance, extracted his bag, and locked up, scanning his surroundings furtively as he did so, but no one was paying him the slightest heed. He strolled out of the car park with the unhurried, patent, virtue of the high wage tradesman in plenty of time for work, and made for the down side of the crossing. Pausing momentarily on the pavement, he looked, unanxiously, back up the road leading to London. Then, as if satisfied, he moved into a shop doorway, laid the bag down between his parted feet, and lit his pipe. The smoke was hot and rank on his foodless palate but he kept it going. Loitering always carried some risk but not too much if you filled out the picture artistically — the punctual workman, his kit at his feet, calmly enjoying his after breakfast pipe while he waited for the firm's minivan to take him and his mates to the building site on the Basingstoke road. You saw him every work-a-day morning, if you were unlucky enough to be up so early.

Lynch knew he was standing at the level crossing on a series of assumptions. Assumption One was that Smith-Heritage and Ramsden had taken his bait, and would try to kill him at Runneymede, and damn the consequences. Assumption Two was that Smith-Heritage had spent the night at home and would cross the level crossing to get to Runneymede. Assumption Three was that Smith-Heritage would want to be in the field early but not too early; he would want to cut down the risk of being flushed out of his hide by a bladderful mongrel and its pendant owner. By his reckoning he should be passing him between seven and half past. He hoped that the gates would be open. A lynx-eyed campaigner sitting for five minutes with nothing to do but stare, and nothing to stare at but a workman in a doorway, could discomfit that same workman into uncharacteristic action.

Just after seven a white Jaguar XJ6 floated effortlessly over the gleaming parallels, Smith-Heritage gentling it like a father with his toddler on reins. Again he was dressed differently, this time in a dark zip-up windproof, tight at the neck. But there was no mistaking that barrelled torso, the ruthless prow of a face, the knife edged widow's peak. The hunt was up and the hunter was abroad.

The passenger seat was empty as was the back seat. Where the hell was Ramsden? The car had to be Ramsden's, so where was the owner? Was he to be picked up en route? Was he to follow in the Aston Martin? Or was it that the cautious Colonel was looking to his flanks and making sure that his car wasn't going to be anywhere near any crime, past, present, or to come. Lynch reassured himself: Ramsden, with paper bag, would not want to make the rendezvous too early; he would want to drive into the car park at Runneymede, conspicuously, laudably, on time.

But, as time trotted by, his confidence thinned to vanishing point. Maybe his gossamer structure of lies and bluff had simply collapsed of its own frailty. Maybe Smith-Heritage had been bent on nothing more sinister than fresh mushrooms for breakfast; or getting the Jag's plugs cleaned at a busy garage; or putting his name down soonest for a Council house. Maybe this, maybe that.

By twenty-five past seven his doubts had flowered into nagging, ulcerating anxiety; no Aston Martin, no Ramsden, no returning white XJ6, no nothing except increased activity around him.

Sunningdale was shucking off its continental quilts, parking its cars, flourishing its season tickets. Newsagents were carting stringed, pink bundles of Financial Timeses into their shops.

He decided that he could not afford to wait another minute. Hoisting the toolbag, he started walking in the direction of Blythswood Drive. After fifty yards the drag on his right arm forced him to abandon the light infantry pace and settle for a dignified slow march. Filling a toolbag on the 'you never know' principle was fine, so long as you didn't have to carry the damned thing. It was going to be a taxing stroll.

It was a quarter to eight when he eventually heaved himself into the drive of Number 32, his eyes blinded with sweat, the bag threatened to tear his arm off at the oxter. The first thing he saw was the Aston Martin anchored outside the front door, cold, unmanned. Ramsden wasn't going to be driving that into the Runneymede car park just before eight o'clock, though what good that snippet of knowledge was doing him he couldn't think. Thankfully, he unlocked his cramped fingers and let the bag sink on to the front step with a clanking thud. Then he put a knuckle to the bell push and held it there for the metallic resonance to shrill through the closed up house, plangent, demanding. Nothing stirred within.

Perhaps friend Ramsden was having a cosy lie in in the guest room while master fetched the morning papers and fresh jam for the first butty of the day. He tried again, pressing, releasing, pressing again; and stealing a quick glance behind him as he did so. Nobody. The postman had cycled past him with a cheery good morning, ten minutes earlier, and was now well up the Drive beyond Number 32.

Still no answer. No splash of bare feet on cold lino, no 'gardez-loo' of protestant profanity from a flung back upper window. There was nobody home.

He lifted the bag again, this time with his left hand, and walked, right, across the front of the house, then turned left up the side to the rear of the garage. The solid access door was locked, secure. From the bag he drew out the thin mesh gloves with the reinforced finger pads and pulled them on. The jemmy was pleasantly cold through the thin fabric as he attacked the door, levering savagely, time too precious for craftsmanship.

The aluminium ladder was featherlight after the wrenching density of the toolbag. He shouldered it round to the back of the house at a staggering run, manoeuvred it until the top rung rested just below the wide, uncurtained picture window on the upper floor. Fetching the toolbag round at speed, he fed from it, into the capacious pockets of his overalls, the things he would need aloft. Then he clambered up.

It would be out of character, he had reasoned, for Smith-Heritage not to have set his burglar alarm on leaving the empty house. And it was certainty that the alarm would be efficient, and silent. One teensy-weensy knife blade illicit in any window frame and the tocsin would sound all round the local cop shop. Before an unsuspecting intruder had one leg over the sill a grinning sergeant would be feeling his collar, benevolently. There was, however, a fair chance that pressure on the glass of the upper floor windows would NOT activate the alarm as it did in some sophisticated systems. One way or another, he was going to find out. Of course, the assault on the garage could well have catapulted a panda car in his direction already, but he was fairly sure the garage had been 'clean'.

He put his hand against the window to steady himself.

The rectangular, glass sheet measured approximately 8 feet by 6. The quickest way in was to smash it, and another glance at his watch tempted him, sorely, but uncontrolled fragmentation referred through to the frame might just trigger the alarm. Whereas the pressure that a window cleaner would exert — there was a thought — window cleaners again! Had the ungallant Colonel, idly following a weaving shammy on this very window, been seized suddenly, like a criminous James Watt, with an inspired entry into the treasury of Brace and Clelland. Not that it mattered. He extended the jointed carpenter's rule, planted it firmly against the glass and took out the black marking pen at the same moment as he heard the milk float rattle into the drive in front of the house.

This was unmistakably 'Tradesman's Entrance' country; no plonking the bottles on the front door step and a saucy 'Hello, darlin!' to the becurlered chatelaine here.

He glanced down. The kitchen door was right of centre, but only just. If the milkman came round the house by the garage side there was no way he could miss the wreckage of the garage back door.

It had been one of the great sadnesses of Lynch's boyhood that, unlike every single one of his peers, he had never learned to, or been able to, whistle. His was never the piercing fluting that cleared the tanner ba' footballers off the street in advance of the unsporting polis; at no time in his greenscarved adolescence had he ever been able to swell the two fingered bugling that greeted the sacrilege of a blue jersey on the Parkhead pitch. He couldn't whistle now, either.

He sang the first verse of 'The Mountains of Mourne'; he only knew the first verse.

Suddenly there were measured steps on the flags below, and synchronous clankings — from the right.

'Happy in your work, mate?'

Lynch moved the rule into a perpendicular position, 'Better'n listenin' to the wife moanin' about the electricity bills.'

The milkman laughed. 'All the same, aren't they. Guv'nor about?'

'Went out when I arrived.'

Lynch didn't look down; he could hear two bottles being deposited, one after the other, by the kitchen door.

'Say anything about eggs?'

He drew his black lines with a steady hand; the man below couldn't see what he was doing very clearly.

'Not to me,' he called down.

'Sometimes had eggs on a Thursday. Doesn't matter. What's up with the window, then?'

'Nothing,' replied Lynch 'Just wants tinted glass instead. Wants it today, too.

You know how it is round here.'

'I know,' sympathised the milkman, 'All bleedin' Paul Gettys. Ah, well. Must get on. Mind how you go.'

'You too,' sang out Lynch, as the other jangled his way back round to the float. He snatched another look at his watch — one minute to eight.

From inside his overalls he took out the rubber suction pad, the handle of which he had cut down to nine inches the day before. He applied it to the black oblong he had just outlined on the glass — three feet by four, just big enough to admit him, and big enough to be awkward to handle. Lining the rule up again on his black markings he ran the glass cutter along each side — twice for good measure. He pulled gently on the suction pad; it still gripped. He began to push on it now, lightly but steadily until the incised portal gave before him, rasping, gritty, and he was through, the cut out pane still sticking to the suction pad. He doubted that it would hold for long. Quickly, but delicately, he lowered the fragile mortar board inwards and to the right until it came to rest on the gold broadloom carpet. He had a fleeting glimpse of a wide four poster with a brocaded canopy, Regency wall paper, a white door straight in front, before he pulled his trunk back out and skittered down again to the ground.

Once down he swung the ladder away from the wall, extended it by a couple of rungs, and then let it fall back. Now the top was proud of the sill of his improvised wicket gate. Up again in a trice with the bag which he tossed in and then followed through like a triple jumper, one foot on the white glossed, interior.

It struck him as he landed that if fingerprints could be latent then so could footprints; so farewell chukka boots! Pity!

Scooping up the bag, like a pigsticker at the gallop, he jerked open the bedroom door, took the upstairs hall in three highstepping strides, and plunged down the thickly carpeted staircase.

The telephone rested on a long walnut table on the right side of the square entrance hall. Awkwardly, with his gloved finger, he spun the dial round three times.

'Police. Hurry!'

'Sunningdale Police Station here. Can — '

'There's a madman at the Kennedy Memorial, with a gun.' He shouted breathlessly; he was indeed breathless. 'Just shot at me from the trees. All I was doing was walking the dog.'

'If you'll just give me your name sir and the number from which — '

'He hit me in the arm. I've got to get to a hospital. Hurry!'

Lynch slammed the receiver down and pushed his cuff back for the umpteenth time. Twelve minutes past. A seven a.m. rendezvous would have been safer, he realised now, but hindsight would be no shield for the innocent who might, this minute, be bending down to peek into a lonely white carrier bag on the flank of Runneymede Hill. He could only hope that the police would arrive before it happened.

Still panting, he took the stairs two at a time and ran back to the wounded window. Leaning out, he grabbed the ladder, angled it right, and let it drop. It hit the terrace with a clatter and slid inwards until it stopped against the wall. A standing ladder always drew eyes upwards, and where there were milkmen there would be bakers, and greengrocers, and fishmongers. Smith-Heritage wouldn't be one for pushing trolleys round supermarkets. Whereas who paid any attention to a ladder on the ground? Well, that was the theory.

He would like to have grafted the cut-out back with the transparent tape he had pocketed for just that purpose but that was a finicky task that would consume minutes he might not have to spare. The police would make a frontal headlong dash on Runneymede, engines flat out, sirens screaming, punching noise at the reported sniper to deflect his aim, blunt his frenzy. If Smith-Heritage and associate were still there at the first banshee wail and managed to get away clear, Lynch could have twenty, twenty five minutes to play with. But suppose some early risen tourist on a tight package deal had kept tryst with his late President at five past eight. The white

Jaguar could be racing towards Sunningdale at that very moment. Dalliance could be fatal.

Since he was already on the upper floor a quick recce wouldn't sacrifice too many precious seconds. The room he was standing in was obviously sir's. A silk dressing gown lay, neatly folded, on the flounced coverlet cloaking the ample bed; soft, calfskin slippers stood, precisely dressed on the floor below it. An octagonal marquetry table, by the bed, supported a silver tray carrying a brandy bottle, a balloon glass; an open book, face down, nudged an ivory cigarette box and an onyx table lighter. There was a sprinkle of ash in a veined agate tray the size of a soup plate.

The black marble fireplace was imitation Adam, but good imitation; while the merry carriage clock on its mantelshelf was undoubtedly genuine. Lynch didn't know about the seascapes on the walls, but they were originals so they were probably worth a bob or two.

The master bedroom. And master wasn't going in for hair shirts this year.

He opened the other doors along the hall. Two bathrooms, a lavatory, an overflowing linen cupboard, three other bedrooms — luxurious but with the dry cold feel of the rarely opened. A lone ranger, like himself.

On his way back along the hall a sudden thought kicked him in the diaphragm and drove him back into the main bedroom. The rubber plunger! With his prints of the day before all over it! That was the kind of forgetfulness that overcrowded Parkhurst. He was never going to wear the mantle of a Moriarty.

With his evilly honed pocket knife he prised it away from the adherent glass, and hared downstairs to replace it in the bulging hold-all. At the same time he took out the Colt and the cartridges and loaded it on the hall table. His stint in the Boy Scouts was paying off at last.

The roomy hall was panelled, head-high, with wood that glowed like amber. A bulky grandfather clock tocked the morning away, sonorously, beside an open door on his left, leading into the sitting room. On the right of the front door, facing him, a solid wooden box was leeched to the wall, five feet from the floor — the alarm control. A brass key-hole twinkled in the Lilliputian barrier. Probably a duel system: the front door key would switch on and off as the householder left, and returned; and, at night, it would be set from the box.

He turned and set out to explore the corridor behind him that led to the rear of the house — cloakroom, study, breakfast room, larder, kitchen — all empty.

He came back and went into the sitting room — a York stone fireplace at the gable end, a monstrous television set between the windows overlooking the front garden, chintz covered chairs and settees, occasional tables, floor lamps, bookcases, a gilt newspaper carrier. At the back wall, facing the windows, was an ormolu writing table as wide as a fives court, and behind it reared up a throne of ancient, blackened wood, with a bright scarlet cushion. Against the wall on the right of the doorway, a massive Jacobean dresser, reaching for the ceiling, was ablaze with bottles, decanters and crystal glasses. Nobody was going to go thirsty in this house, thought Lynch.

He went across the hall and opened the door into the dining room — a curvaceous dining table, eight tapestried arm-chairs, a bow fronted sideboard. But food was secondary here; this was not a shrine to Epicurus so much as a temple of Mars, for every spare piece of wall space offered some tribute or other to the god of muzzle velocity. Annie could certainly get her gun here.

Glass fronted cases paraded shotguns, hunting rifles, target rifles, antiques, small hand guns. There were firearms in sprayed fans badging the walls, a mounted square of blunderbusses, rosettes of bayonets, ancient and modern. The sideboard was bouffant with trophies — cups, salvers, vases, bowls, tankards — all applauding the Colonel's sharp eye and steady trigger finger.

In black and white, and inglorious technicolor, the camera had snared him, at club shoots, on ranges, in uniform, in mufti; smug over a gralloched royal stag;

ankle deep in corpsed pheasant; pugareed astride a glassy-eyed tiger. No photograph, however, of a fair-curled girl, with a glittering bauble on her breast, lifeless on an English green. Degree of difficulty minus one.

Lynch knew a little about guns; he could venture a maker's name to the long, slender barrelled snaphaunce high on on the interior wall; he could identify the pair of over-and-under tap action pocket pistols below it; but in the shop window of a master gunner like this he felt he should be wearing L-plates. However, he did recognise one unexpected item in a glassed-in montage of assorted small arms — a Chinese Army silenced pistol.

'And you,' he addressed it, 'wherever you came from, might be just the wee boy, if the worst comes to the worst!'

With his elbow he shattered the glass and lifted out the stubby gun. Above it was a dusty, dainty outline which pricked and teased at the memory before he placed it. The display cabinet rested on a stout unglazed, matching cupboard which was also locked. Returning to the hall he liberated the jemmy once again and came back to rip open the defiant twin doors without the benefit of advanced lock smithery. The ammunition was neatly stacked in labelled cartons and he found what he was hoping for immediately: a box marked '.32' with an inked in bracket 'TYPE 64 LOW POWDER'.

He checked the action of the pistol.

'Clean, bright, and slightly oiled,' he muttered. 'That's a good little soldier boy.'

Reckless of the looking glass patina of the dining table he spilled out the cartridges on it and loaded. He remembered what the gun dealer had said of the assassin's friend he was holding: 'Very good for close quarter work, sir, but limited penetration beyond forty yards.'

If the worst did come to the worst he would take damn good care to be much nearer than forty yards.

On his way back to the sitting room he replaced the jemmy and took the bag with him.

The writing table was every bit as

heavy as it looked, but in easy stages, he swivelled it round until it was at right angles to the back wall, and facing the open door. If there had to be shooting he wanted full frontal targets not silhouettes.

The black chair of state felt as if it might be ballasted by a twin of the Stone of Scone but, with much protesting from his stomach muscles he managed to lift and drag it to a position behind the writing table.

He placed the Chinese Type 64 behind the elaborate antique writing set, took the Colt out of his pocket and put it there as well. Two guns were better than one, he reflected, though in this house he wouldn't have said no to a howitzer and a Chieftain tank.

He sat down, thankfully, on the scarlet cushion. His watch showed eight thirty five. He was as ready as he would ever be.

If the law had been quick enough and lucky enough to tag the troops in ambuscade it would hold them until it had checked the weaponry that Lynch was certain would be found on them. Smith-Heritage would have every permit, licence, and laissez-passer known to man; and pull and prestige as well. But where guns were in sight the police were always canny and painstaking.

If they didn't arrive back at nine o'clock, he would get Price-Carruthers on the job to find out whether the unlikely partners were 'helping the police with their inquiries'. If they were, then he would name them to the lawyer as the murderers of Valerie Scott; the police would listen to Price-Carruthers even if they didn't like him. Why was he so sure the police didn't like him?

And if the police didn't have them?

Then it would have to be 'Fallback Plan B' which rested on some ungentle coercion. How would Ramsden be, under duress? No need to speculate about the Colonel: that one wouldn't crack under a steam hammer, if Lynch was any judge. But Ramsden now? Could this tongue be made to wag just a little?

But then, even if he did cough?

In the heyday of his upper bracket snooping, Lynch used to keep a set of

Law books on his office desk, partly to impress the clients, partly to let him know exactly which law he was about to break in pursuance of his avocation. Quite often, when business was less than brisk he would browse through them on the principle that it never did any harm to know what the other side were up to.

Now, as he sat, waiting, on the black throne he could see the printed lines in his mind's eye:

'The essence of a confession is that it should have been made to someone in authority over criminal proceedings — a policeman, a magistrate, a prosecutor.' And how did an ex-con get himself elevated into that stratum? But perhaps if it was in writing! There was plenty of flash writing paper on the writing table in front of him. Give each a sheet of paper, dictate the confessions, get each one to sign, witness and date them both himself, then dial 999. Simple!

Except that the text on confessions went on a bit:

'A confession is inadmissible unless it

was voluntary, and a confession will only be held to have been voluntary if it was not made in consequence of a threat — '

Did a loaded pistol pointed in the general direction of the large intestine count as a threat? Judges could be pernickety about a thing like that. Still, that was their worry, not Lynch's.

There was a crumb of comfort further on, too!

'Facts discovered in consequence of an inadmissible confession may be proved, provided that there is no need to refer to the terms of the confession.' So even if the confession was inadmissable as evidence, the police could chase up the facts at their leisure, with help from Kleenglass, Lynch, Imperial Car, Uncle Tom Cobley and all.

But what about that little scorpion of a codicil:

' — in many instances the subsequently discovered facts are devoid of probative value if no reference is made to the confession.'

So, where would that leave Regina v. Ramsden and Smith-Heritage? He had no idea; and he was willing to wager a pony that my Lords of Appeal in Ordinary, whoever they were, had no idea either. All in all, he doubted whether there was a lot of mileage to be got from Fallback Plan 'B' though it would have to be attempted.

Which left only 'Last Resort Plan C'.

But was it not always thus? Was it not the Second Law of Sod that 'Where there are two easy ways, and one hard way to achieve your end, the two easy ways must always prove to be delusive'.

'And how about that, Pascal, for an early morning pensee?' he asked, silently. And on an empty stomach, too! And blood sugar dropping so low it must be nearly out of sight!

He followed, with his eyes, a pair of blackbirds pecking their way intently, across the shaven, emerald lawn. Obviously, they had a signed chitty from the Colonel authorising them to feed there, or they wouldn't have presumed.

He squirmed in his seat and tried to think pure thoughts. He hoped, earnestly, that it would not take too long for

Smith-Heritage and Ramsden to surface somewhere; he didn't think his blood sugar would take kindly to the idea of going without lunch as well.

19

They came at five minutes to nine.

From where he sat he followed the Jaguar up the drive until it came to a halt beside the Aston Martin. Smith-Heritage switched off and got out of the car in one lithe athletic movement for so big a man. From the back seat he lifted out the rod case, the brown canvas bag which he slung over his shoulder and the leather binocular case which he draped round his neck. The car keys he tossed at Ramsden, straightening up on the other side, a white carrier bag in his left hand. He was dressed as Lynch had seen him from the Mary Hoy: green windcheater, dark trousers. Smith-Heritage, below the zip-up tunic which Lynch had glimpsed at the Sunningdale level crossing was trousered in charcoal grey, and his feet were encased in heavy black brogues.

'Daddy's gone a hunting!' muttered Lynch.

They disappeared from view; there was the double click of the lock as Smith-Heritage opened the front door.

'Of course they'll check it out, Ramsden: it was the only car in the car park. So what? Stolen Surbiton, abandoned at Runneymede.'

'Aye. Like as not they'll think some daft lads wi' too much ale. The whistle was a good idea; if it hadn't been — '

The doorway into the sitting room was wide enough so they came in together and stopped dead at the sight of gun steady in Lynch's right hand. Below the binocular case on his chest, Smith-Heritage wore a blue riband from which dangled a referee's black whistle.

'Who ta bloody hell?' exploded Ramsden.

'Chummy, Ramsden; clever, clever chummy who put us at Runneymede, then sicked the police on to us. Right?'

'Bull's eye as usual, Colonel,' affirmed Lynch.

He pointed the Chinese gun at the bigger man's groin, 'You stay absolutely still, Colonel. You, Ramsden take three paces to the right. That's a good lad. Now one pace forward. Wouldn't have done for Caterham barracks, would it, Colonel? Never mind. Do exactly as I tell you or it's tiny tummyaches for two. Now Ramsden, drop the paper bag. What's in it by the way? Sliced Sunday Supplements? Not that it matters.'

'That's my gun!' shouted Smith-Heritage, in shocked dismay, 'You've been at my guns! Bloody vandal! I hope you know what you're doing.'

'I hope so, too, sir. Now hand the fishing rods to Ramsden. Hold the case at arm's length. Now take off the fishing bag and drop it behind your back, and the binoculars. Carefully, now. You wouldn't want me to get nervous. Good. Now fold your arms across your chest — the way angels do it, or corpses. Palms flat. That's it. Hardly St Anthony of Padua but you haven't had the practice.'

Smith-Heritage stood rigid, his whole being absorbed in Lynch, the mute, hot fury coming across in waves so that Lynch imagined he could feel the seething blast.

'You, Ramsden, hold the case out at as far as you can. With your other hand take hold of the bottom and tip everything out on to the floor.'

Up-ended the container yielded its contents stickily: two tapered rods in sections, overtaken by something shorter, solider, which thumped heavily on the carpet — a firearm.

Ramsden dropped the empty bag beside its contents and snapped his arms back to his sides.

'Now, Ramsden!' barked the Colonel, 'Now, man!'

Ramsden got his right arm up to thirty degrees as Lynch fired — two echo-less plops, the bullets punching small holes in the green windcheater over the heart. Ramsden pitched back, his head crashing against the dresser and setting the winking bottles aquiver. A small object slid from his hand as he fell, coming to rest beside the rod case.

There was silence for a long moment. Smith-Heritage did not shift his eyes from Lynch's face; his breathing was even, regular.

'You can say an ave for your partner, if you like, Colonel but don't do anything else.'

'Dead?'

Lynch nodded, 'You wouldn't mark me high on my grouping but he's dead alright. I didn't think Derringers existed outside Hollywood but I spotted the empty outline in your gun case. Didn't expect it to be with him, though. You are a pretty crafty brigand, Colonel, that you are. I thought they might snaffle you at the Memorial but you do manage to stay ahead of the game, don't you? How did it go? Ramsden drives the stolen car to the car park and walks up with the paper bag; you drive the Jag up on to the hill behind and come down from above. When the sirens sound you toot on your little whistle and Ramsden comes up again, through the trees, over the fence and back to the Jag and you're away. Kept your line of retreat open. You must have been a hell of a battalion commander in your day.'

The other said nothing, just kept on staring fixedly at Lynch. There was something flawed in the immaculate, almost dandified appearance that the Colonel presented even in a zip-up tunic, Lynch saw: the right cuff was tight to the wrist, the left was loose as if the elastic had given way. Bachelordom had its penalties, as Lynch had discovered — no little woman, with needle at the ready, bearing down on the loose thread, the missing button.

'That gun from the rod case, that's not the one you used on Valerie Scott is it?'

Smith-Heritage's face remained impassive; if the name meant anything to him he wasn't showing it.

'You put her down with a .303 rifle. That looks like a Delisle Silenced Carbine.'

'You know guns, Mr er — '

'Lynch. Pat Lynch. A little but not in your class, Colonel.'

'Not many are. You were a Jock or I miss my guess. Damned good soldiers. I was brigaded with them once.'

'About the only thing we could agree on, I fancy. I suppose the Carbine would have vanished like the .303 — totally?'

'You realise, Lynch, that you have

murdered a man. You may of course plead self defence. However, there's the breaking and entering bit, killing in the commission of a crime. Still, a good silk might do something with the Derringer if you told the whole story as you see it.'

'As they used to say in 'oor' street 'Away aff, Colonel'. I'll need a great big chanty fu' o' silks to make the jury believe self defence, even if it is true. To make sense they'll also have to believe that you murdered Valerie Scott, and that you were all set to knock me off with that Carbine on the floor at the Kennedy Memorial.'

'Why there, by the way?'

'It was an excellent spot for your purpose, you'll admit, and so it was a good spot for mine. There was also a subconscious reason that I didn't realise for quite a while: it was as close as I could get to the scene of Valerie Scott's death without arousing your suspicions as to what I was really up to. Poetic justice?'

'You were in that boat, weren't you?'

Lynch nodded.

'I didn't care for that boat at that place at that time.'

'You went to the boatyard, then?'

'I didn't care either for that yarn you left there but I couldn't do much about it; you were pushing me for time.'

'Still, you didn't miss much.'

'I missed enough; you're here, in my house. There is one thing, though, my charlady's due here at eleven o'clock; I wouldn't want her harmed and I'm sure you wouldn't, so — '

Lynch shook his head reprovingly, 'Wednesdays and Saturdays, Wednesdays and Saturdays. I try not to miss anything, either.'

'So I see.' The voice and features were still controlled, 'Then let us get down to the central issue — your interest in my affairs. Money I suppose. The usual have-not trying to subtract from the have.'

Lynch gazed at him, pityingly, 'I bet they noticed that weakness at Staff College.'

The black eyebrows tightened angrily over the eagle beak and the colour purpled on the skin taut over the cheekbones; Lynch had struck a nerve.

'What the hell are you talking about?'

'Empathy — the lack of. Your inability to put anyone, even your enemy in anything but your own shoes. The inability to put yourself in his shoes. Oh, I'm a have-not alright, but it's justice or retribution or revenge I'm after. So, don't worry about your money. Two years ago you killed a girl, Valerie Scott at Engle — '

'Nonsense! You don't have one shred of evidence.'

'Eleven days ago her father hired me to find her killer,' continued Lynch, 'and — '

'How could he? He's dead — ' Smith-Heritage bit the word off too late.

'Oh Colonel! A slip. Not like you. You wouldn't, shouldn't, have known of Richard Scott or that he was dead unless you had an interest. But you're right; he is dead. He hired me posthumously, you might say. If you were an imaginative man you might feel the dead hand reaching out from the grave to clutch your throat. No? I didn't think so — always the pragmatist.'

'Neither you, nor anyone else will ever

find a single piece of evidence to connect me to any crime whatsoever. You may be assured of that.'

'Oh, I am, sir, I am. You're good, damned good. But what about our deceased friend lying there? You don't think he might have got his fingers caught in the mangle once or twice?'

'Perhaps,' Smith-Heritage shrugged. 'I knew him as the owner of a prosperous club in Manchester which I visited occasionally. He needed capital for expansion; I have capital; I invited him here to talk about it. You shot him.'

'And you will have witnesses and correspondence to back that story up, I'm sure, for you're very thorough. I wonder how many villainous pies you have your greedy little thumb in. How many Ramsdens are there on your payroll? There's more than that poor sod working for you, I'll wager. And it's not just the money is it? Though you like that.'

'I like money; I have money.'

'Yes, but you didn't have when you retired I would think — just your pension and a half colonel's pension wouldn't run to all this. You needed more than that, a lot more. More important, perhaps, you needed action, risk. You had been on a diet for twenty-five years of excitement, danger, killing, bloodletting and suddenly it was withdrawn. A man like you, living at the top of your bent, no, you couldn't take cold turkey.'

'What exactly,' asked the colonel in a bored voice, 'do you want of me? If I wanted psycho-therapy I should go to Harley Street.'

'Good question. I've got a good answer. Just your signature. Not much, really. Think about what you put your signature on — cheques, receipts, chits for drinks at your clubs, letters, Christmas cards.'

'Signature to what? Incidentally, besides being rather silly, this posture is wearisome. Do you mind if I put my arms down?'

Lynch's index finger tightened, 'This trigger doesn't take a lot of pressure. Did you know that? Yes, I mind. Keep the arms across the chest and the palms flat, just like those dead warriors you see in cathedrals. Good. I've taken the liberty of writing this out on your own stationery and I'm going to read it out and then you can sign it — or not. That's fair enough, isn't it?'

The other stared at him pensively but said nothing.

Lynch read aloud from the paper in front of him.

> 'I confess that at Englefield Green on the 15th of May, 1975 I shot and killed Valerie Scott. I did this because of the possibility that she had recognised and might later identify my associate, Joseph Ramsden with whom I robbed Brace and Clelland, Builders, of Staines of £90,000 on the 28th of August, 1975.'

He looked up. 'That's it, Colonel, not a lot really. You sign it and date it and I witness it. Then I dial 999 and we take it from there.'

'Even if I sign this you still can't get out of being charged with the killing of Ramsden. And you have no surety that I'd be a witness for your defence.'

'Somebody said the only sure things

were death and taxes. I take my chance.'

'And if I don't sign?'

'Then I'm left with two choices: dial 999 anyway and present the police with you and Ramsden — he can be connected to Valerie, to Kleenglass and to Brace and Clelland. Valerie was killed by a marksman, you are a marksman and he's in your house.'

'Thinnish — the connection to me I mean. How about Ramsden and I finding you in the house in the act of robbery and you shoot Ramsden?'

'And leave you alive while I give myself up?'

'Horror, remorse at the unintentional shooting, it would add substance to your story of a regrettable accident. There are any number of scenarios. I wonder which scripts would be accepted, yours or mine.'

'Yours, I think. But a signed confession, even one made under duress, might give me a better chance, that's all.'

'And your second choice?'

Lynch stared at him stonily.

'I execute you here for the murder of Valerie Scott.'

Smith-Heritage gave a slight derisive snort 'Come now, Lynch. Shooting Ramsden was one thing, but cutting down a completely defenceless stranger in cold blood while he's standing in front of you absolutely helpless that takes bottle. Think you've got it?'

'We'll have to find out, shan't we.'

'So, I'm on a hiding to nothing. If I sign you call the police. If I don't sign you either call the police or you kill me, but I don't know which until I've made my decision. Russian Roulette with only two chambers.'

'More exciting that way. That should appeal to you.'

'Oh. I sign.'

'Sensible chap! Don't move yet. I don't want you within five yards of me.'

The swarthy face in front of Lynch lit up with sudden glee? 'I frighten you?'

'You do just that. All you divine-right-to-rule-and-be-rich bastards frighten me, but you, you're way out in front. You scare the piss out of me. So stay still and do as I say.'

The alert eyes glinted with amusement.

'You're very persuasive.'

'I'm going to toss your leather blotting pad over to your feet. The confession is tucked into a corner. But don't do anything till I tell you. Got it?'

'Sir!' barked Smith-Heritage still grinning.

Lynch skimmed the stiff foot square blotting pad across the floor; it struck the other's right foot and lay on the carpet.

'When I give you the word, but not before, I want you to kneel down and affix your signature to the confession, your usual signature.'

'How will you know it's my usual signature?'

Lynch held up three envelopes, torn open, 'These tradesmen's bills were for posting today, I assume. I took another liberty: I opened them.'

The colonel's eyes widened appreciatively, 'The cheques. Of course. You're quite bright — for a Jock.'

'Och aye! They say we'll be ready for the alphabet soon.'

'One small thing. I don't have a pen on me.'

Lynch looked carefully, suspiciously at the strong feral figure, made ridiculous by the incongruity of the piously crossed arms, tense, tight as a bow-string.

'Somehow I didn't think you would have.'

He lifted a plastic biro from the desk in front of him, 'I'll throw this across.'

'What do I do? Catch it with my teeth?'

'Don't be silly. Here. Catch.'

Lynch threw the black, almost weightless, cylinder at the colonel's face. The reflexes were a teenager's not a middle-aged man's, the right hand catching the pen at arm's length, the left hand dropping to the seam of the trousers and rising. And that was the one Lynch was concentrating on.

Two wine corks popped within milliseconds of each other and Smith-Heritage grimaced in shocked spasm as two small dark craters opened up in his zip-up tunic.

'Christ Almighty! You — you shot me!' the last words cracked falsetto in agonised disbelief.

Lynch couldn't speak, he could only sit

and watch as the bulky figure moved towards him like a great wounded animal, suffering and enraged. The full lips were drawn over the gums, the tongue thrust out like a board as the strong teeth came down, clenched, locked, and blood stained the white enamel.

One step, a second — faltering. The distended brown eyes fixed balefully on Lynch in a deadly concentration of hate and purpose.

Without warning the legs gave and he fell forward on to his hands and knees, still trying desperately with scrabbling finger to point the miniscule weapon in his left hand.

Lynch sat paralysed, his gun hand frozen to the desk, impotent, sick to his gut at the spectacle of a great beast dying — hard. Then it was over as the Colonel crumpled face down on the carpet, stilled and shrunken like a puppet put by.

'What a tricky, savage little soldier boy you turned out to be,' muttered Lynch, hoarsely. 'Two Derringers, not one; sacrificing Ramsden just to draw me off the scent; left hand, right hand — kill with either, and you nearly had me, Colonel. My God, you nearly had me and I couldn't have fired a third shot at you — not even to save my life.'

He started to rise but his limbs were water and he collapsed back into the chair. The Chinese gun slipped from the slack useless fingers and clattered on to the desk top, as the bile rose up in his throat, sour and scalding. He rested his limp, nerveless arms on the cold surface of the desk, pillowed his forehead on them and closed his eyes.

He had never killed two men in one morning before; it was not an easy thing to do.

20

He was in the ring at Catterick Camp eyeing his opponent on the stool opposite. Around him was the shuffle of Army boots, the heaving of khaki elbows and shoulders, the running motor throb of expectant voices, hoarse against the swelling curlicues of tobacco smoke. The Staff P.T.I. who was going to referee was looking at him pityingly from a neutral corner. No wonder! Somebody had got the weights mixed up. The big bruiser opposite had two stones on him — at least. The zip-up tunic wasn't fooling Lynch. The hidden voice behind his right ear was insistent, 'He's slow, Pat, must be. In — out. Go for the flab in the middle. That's what the tunic's for, hiding it. Go for the flab in the middle. In — out, Pat. You can take him.'

The bell went, shrill, clangorous, and went, and kept on ringing and ringing. What the hell was the time-keeper up to?

Lynch awoke to reality and the telephone in the hall behind him. Awoke from what? Sleep? Faint? Black-out? He wasn't sure. How long had it been? He looked at his watch. Ten minutes, perhaps. No more.

The strident whirring finally stopped, and quiet mantled the house again, metronomed by the tick-tock from the grandfather clock. He worked his arms and shoulders; there was tone and feeling back in the muscles, now.

A new sound broke the orchestrated quiet as a baker's van rolled up to the front of the house. The roundsman got out, pulled up the shutter and put two loaves in a basket.

'Wholemeal,' observed Lynch, idly, to himself. 'The Colonel likes his roughage.'

The back door bell rang twice, somewhere behind him, but he didn't move. The vanman came into view again, tossed the empty basket in, rolled down the shutter, and jumped into the cab. Lynch watched, detached, removed, as the van moved smoothly down the drive and vanished.

He shifted his gaze to the two bodies on the floor, the white carrier bag. He had a feeling that he ought to be doing something but he couldn't for a moment think what it was. He eased himself out of the wooden chair, went into the hall and sat down on the second step. He got his pipe going after five ineffectual tries with fingers uncontrollably trembling. He sat and smoked and tried desperately to pull his head together, and, eventually, he did, and everything around became sharper, harder. The zoom lens in the camera suddenly focussing.

He laid out his options.

They weren't many.

He could call the police. And explain?

But no matter how or why they do it, the fact is that people who kill other people usually have to go to jail for doing so. Particularly, people who have hardly been out of jail for five minutes.

So, scrub that option.

He could simply walk away.

And before you could say 'Jack the Ripper' the faces of Smith-Heritage and Ramsden would be framed in all the dailies and millions of television screens. And what would poor Frances do then, poor thing? She had heard the name Ramsden before, hadn't she? And what of the Manager of Imperial Car Insurance? Hadn't the name come up quite recently? And that tycoon manque of the window cleaning jungle, the embittered, embattled supremo of Kleenglass! He would put another name to that face as quickly as he would wet a sponge. And where would that leave everybody? Back on the doorstep of Patrick Aloysius Cameron Lynch, Esq. that once and future ornament of Her Majesty's Prisons.

Forget it.

He could dispose of the bodies.

It sounded good, simple, a clear, clean solution. Dispose of the bodies! Trouble was he didn't know how to dispose of one body, let alone two. And two was surely more difficult than one.

He could dispose of Ramsden, and leave Smith-Heritage where he lay.

Come to think of it he HAD to dispose of Ramsden's body and Ramsden's car. Ramsden was the link to Valerie, to

Frances, to Imperial Car, to Price-Carruthers, to Lynch. Without him there was nothing to connect himself to the dead soldier. Unless — what about his own suggestion that there would be proof of an innocent business relationship between Ramsden and Smith-Heritage? Not extant, not documented. The Colonel's contacts with a dubious character like Ramsden would have been minimal, verbal, and secret; faced with an obvious bond like the dead man in his sitting room he could and would have improvised speedily and convincingly, but he kept his skirts too clean for there to be an easily uncovered association. Perhaps.

Rightly or wrongly, that seemed to Lynch to be the assumption on which he would have to work.

So the option chose itself — dispose of Ramsden's body and Ramsden's car.

How?

His mind had clicked into gear and was picking up speed at last. Only one way: water.

Years before, he had passed a gravel pit, near Staines, being drained to make way for a reservoir. It had struck him as odd that they should have to take all the water out just so that they could put other water in, months later, but he concluded that they must know what they were doing or they wouldn't be doing it. At the same time he had been surprised at how deep the gravel pit had turned out to be when they scooped the last teaspoonful out.

There were other gravel pits — undrained. Too many, if the local residents were to be believed; they seemed always to be protesting about them to some authority or other — always unsuccessfully, too, it seemed.

So, a gravel pit. Fine. But it couldn't be done before dark and that was some twelve hours away. Spending a balmy summer day with two stiffening cadavers was a prospect falling a little short of idyllic.

Then there was the late military gentleman's private life. Was there a girl friend, or a doting aunt, or a favoured nephew with a front door key, who might decide to drop in for coffee and find a slaughter house, with knacker Lynch missing only the bloody apron? No. The sooner he and Ramsden rid number 32 of their presence the better for all concerned.

Carefully and deliberately he tapped his pipe out in a brass ashtray on the hall table; he had never really believed in Sherlock Holmes's monograph on tobacco ash.

He went back into the sitting room and examined Ramsden's body and the area around it. Flat on his back, the windcheater and the cashmere jumper under it seemed to have absorbed the dead man's blood, totally, Lynch could see none on the carpet. From the right hand trouser pocket he retrieved the car keys; from the floor he lifted the first Derringer and slipped it into his holdall. No point in making life too perplexing for the Regional Crime squad. Then he went upstairs to the linen cupboard.

From its size, the double mattress cover which he brought down must have been a spare for the master's couch.

He laid it out on the uncluttered hall floor and got the scissors from his toolbag. As evenly as his untutored hands could manage he cut down one side and then along the enclosed end so that the cover opened out like the centrefold of a newspaper. Then, gathering it up, he took it into the sitting room and spread it out on the floor beside Ramsden. The edge next to the dead man he pressed and pushed and squeezed under the body. Then he went round to the other side and rolled and wrapped, the way one does a bottle, until Ramsden was completely but loosely in a striped cloth tube. He folded over the top and the bottom, then tied the cylinder down its length at intervals with window cord. Luckily, Ramsden's circulation wouldn't be a problem.

Painstakingly he scrutinised the carpet where the body had lain but there was no trace of blood that he could see.

He went outside.

This was one of the tricky bits. There was no point in wasting time on reconnaissance; either he was going to be lucky or unlucky; either somebody came up the drive or didn't; that was all there was to it.

The Jag responded immediately. He backed, turned, reversed until the rear end of the car was as close to the front door as he could get it. Then he turned off the engine, got out and opened the boot — big enough for a cheese and wine party — Ramsden wouldn't be cramped for space.

Nobody came up the drive.

Back in the sitting room he grasped a circlet of cord and started rolling and manoeuvring the bound body until the had the feet pointing outwards through the sitting room doorway. He lifted the head up and over and got all of the tube into the hall and started rolling again. In life Ramsden hadn't been a bantam: Lynch's muscles were screaming in protest and his sweat was spotting the mattress cover, liberally, as he pushed and rolled and swivelled; the line about Falstaff leapt unbidden into his mind: 'Lards the lean earth as he walks along.'

Finally, one end was protruding from the open front door — the feet by the feel of it. Every sinew was rebelling but he daren't stop for a breather. Bracing his legs on the ground he reached in, grasped the cord below the shoulders and pulled up till he had the top over his shoulders in a clumsy fireman's lift. He spun round awkwardly, and, like a poorly co-ordinated coal heaver, shouldered his meaty burden, clumsily, into the capacious boot. He was never going to be admitted to the Inner Circle of Funeral Directors and Undertakers. He pulled down the lid.

Every aching fibre in him cried out to him to lie down on the grass and suck great gulps of air into his tortured lungs but he kept on going; lose the momentum now and it would take him thirty minutes to get himself moving again. He didn't have thirty minutes to spare.

He tottered back into the sitting room. From the floor behind Smith-Heritage he picked up the thrown blotting pad, rescued the note tucked in the corner and thrust it deep into his shirt breast pocket. He replaced the pad and the pen on the writing table but everything else he left where it had fallen: the rod sections, the case, the carbine, the white carrier bag.

Let the bright young men from the Police College make of the mélange what they would.

Putting the two sets of car keys down on the floor he stripped off the overalls, transferring what he needed to his trouser pockets as he went along. Even in this egalitarian age you didn't see too many plumbers driving to work in an XJ6. The overalls he thrust into his canvas holdall but he kept the gloves on; lots of people wore driving gloves on a hot, sweaty day.

After he lifted the car keys he surveyed the room. Nothing to tag him. He looked a little fearfully at the still corpse of the dead man. Alive it had been the efficient instrument of a self centred human with the magnificent single-mindedness of a great white; dead, it still seemed to menace, or what that just residual terror stamped into Lynch's psyche. He shuddered involuntarily. He was glad it was still.

His legs felt like melting butter as he made his way out of the house, closing the door quietly behind him. He put the hold-all on the floor by the passenger seat and flopped exhausted into the driver's seat; he had hardly enough strength to turn on the ignition let alone turn the steering wheel, but somehow he managed. The car purred into life again and he drove slowly out of the gate leading into number 32. Nothing stirred in Blythswood Drive. He turned right and made his way down towards Sunningdale Station. He still hadn't had breakfast.

21

He never did have breakfast.

But it wasn't till he was parked, late that night, in the dark of Chobham Common, that the fact rose to the surface of his mind. He realised, then, that for the better part of the day, his metabolic apparatus had switched itself over to automatic pilot, enabling all his conscious energy to converge and focus on the logistics of deep-sixing Ramsden. Bully for the sub-conscious.

The local map was liberally speckled with blue patches, but finding the watery slot that combined accessibility with the maximum of privacy had taken most of the day.

Once the spot had been picked the relegation of Ramsden became the kind of problem beloved of Officer Cadet Schools:

'You are in Sunningdale with two cars and a dead body. You are required to insert car with corpse into gravel pit at Chertsey. To minimise the risk of discovery you must wait until midnight to make the deposit. For the same reason you must quit Chertsey immediately on completion of the task, but, by midnight public transport has ceased to operate. You are the officer in charge and the only driver. Make your plan.'

He had.

And now he was sitting in the Jaguar, idly watching the play of headlights deep down in the enclosed canyon of the M3 motorway, and waiting for zero hour.

The dangerous part had been leaving coffined Ramsden all day in the station car park at Sunningdale, broiling. Each time he had checked back he had expected an ashen faced policeman, with a handkerchief over his nose, fiddling at the boot with assorted keys. It hadn't happened.

The awkward part had been sawing through the bramble sleeved fence surrounding the lonely mere, and nose diving into the prickly camouflage every time he heard a car approach. But he needed a gate, and lacerated flesh did heal — eventually.

After that it had been simple shuttling: stashing his own car in Chertsey, then train back to Sunningdale. Next, a dawdling, alcohol-free dinner till dusk cloaked the reclamation of the high powered hearse, and the cautious andante to the libidinous sanctuary of Chobham Common.

The luminous dash-board signalled twenty to twelve. Not long now. The radio was low to the soothing unguent of late night strings; he stood his brain at ease.

Around him, stationary cars loomed like aboriginal humpies — distanced occult. A lighter flared, high to his right, and a girlish laugh peeled out, denying post-coital tristesse.

He sucked at an empty pipe. The internal combustion engine, he reflected, drowsily, as much as the pill, had given a new dimension to wooing. All those hoarded shillings of his salad days, so futilely invested on the back seats of cinema circles. If only he had had a —

The midnight news jerked him out of

his reverie. Bonjour temps perdu! Time to leave the laager.

He drove, carefully, finically, off the Common, motored steadily through Longcross, and a belling from the roused kennels, down on to the Woking-Chertsey road. Speed was the last thing he desired. With his reeking burden nobody would bother about a breathalysing kit.

At Chertsey Bridge, amplified heavy rock pummelled him through the open car window, and a blue light pulsed strobelike from the adit to the tow-path. He hoped the disturbance, whatever it was would keep the force occupied.

Over the river, he angled left on to the unlit capillary he had traversed in the daylight.

On the map, the gravel pit was a mis-shapen ear grafted loosely to the edge of the tarmac. Above the lobe it hung free of the road to leave a broad triangular spit of land, the base trimmed by the wooden fence, the apex piercing the water, a bow-shot to the east.

He slowed down, peering, searching. A hundred yards or so along, his lights picked up the spiky beard he had infiltrated so painfully. Nothing ahead, nothing behind. Pointless to play Hamlet now. Revving up, he spun the wheel right, and charged the barrier at speed. The sheared cross pieces, under the thicket, yielded, crackling and snapping. The barbed vegetation stabbed and ripped the white coachwork. Then he was through, yawing and heaving across the hummocks and crevasses of the stony apron.

Fighting the wilful wheel, he swung half right and bored on, bucking in his seat, till his two marker stakes prodded through the white cone of illumination. When he felt the solidity of brick under him, he braked, doused his lights, killed the engine.

When he had walked the course of the afternoon, he had paused on the fossil floor of a long gone boathouse at the lip of the bank, and cast for the umpteenth time. His lead line of knotted window cord and hammer had found his launching pad.

Now he was ready to fire.

For a couple of minutes he sat,

quiescent, adjusting his eyes to the dark, listening to the bellows of his own lungs.

He released the hand-brake and the car rolled back a yard before he clamped it still again. So much for Hollywood where the villain drove to the cliff edge, pushed with one finger and the Oldsmobile plunged, eagerly, into the Pacific.

Extracting himself, he lifted out the heavy toolbag, placed it clear of the hard standing, and paced the distance from bonnet to water — fifteen yards; he'd need a few more.

Back in the driver's seat he released the brake again and let the vehicle retreat a full car length. It would have to do.

After checking that all the windows were rolled down, he started up, keeping the offside door open with his right elbow. Gingerly, he put the car into gear, and, as it found traction, threw himself out, keeping his left hand on the wheel as his feet fought the ground. For a second he lost his grip. The car veered left, off line. Corkscrewing his trunk back in, he regained the errant tiller and got the car back on course, running alongside, like a royal flunkey, his body in improbably, punishing torque, the swinging door savaging his hip.

Five yards? No yards. The radiator dipping.

As he let go, and drew himself out, the door frame punched him to his hands and knees on the rough paving. Against the backdrop of the luminescent night the bright mass of the XJ6 teetered on the bank like a rifle at the point of balance, it seemed. Tilted, dropped, ponderous as an old warehouse hoist, to jab a great wound in the tensile skin and burrow into the gut of the gravel pit. Water gouted, fell back. Steam curled in a short lived fumarole, the back wheels spun star-flecked droplets high into the air. And then the rupture was healing, the roiled, rippled surface flattening. The Jaguar was gone.

Scrabbling round, he located the toolbag, carried it back in the direction of the road, before hammerthrowing it into the lake, well away from the watery tomb. Even if both his discards were recovered it would take a quantum intuitive leap to link them to each other. He doubted whether even Gibb and Mathews had the cerebral equipment to forge the connection to a dead soldier in Sunningdale.

Making no effort at concealment, he clambered back over the fence, ready to affirm the right of every man to relieve himself in camera. But there was no one to listen. Momentarily, he debated inspecting the breach he had steam-rollered further back, then dismissed the idea. If the flattened hedgerow didn't re-assert itself what was it but the print of a careless motorist, lucky for once?

He started back along the empty road.

The disco was still alive and well when he re-crossed the bridge but the blue light had vanished, he was relieved to see.

There were thirty or so cars strewn round the hotel car park, cyanosed under the spectral arcs that marched the perimeter.

By a bruised mini a figure doubled over, retching in broadcast agony, while a lank haired mentor patted him encouragingly.

'Get it up, Reg. That's favourite.'

From behind a pensioned saloon a

shrill soprano spat. 'Geroff, you horny git! Keep your bleedin' hands to yourself.'

Lynch moved on.

In front of a battered Chevvy a ring of youths sat on the ground, moving in sacramental sequence, a glowing, acrid joint, and a fluted, full bellied flagon. 'Pass the parcel for the big boys?' queried Lynch civilly.

Nobody heard him.

The Sunbeam stood where he had left it, still locked, trim and inviolate under the stark glare.

He got in, rolled down the window and tamped tobacco, loosely, into his cold pipe. In the dance hall the music ceased, and the vacuum filled swiftly with the crash of breaking glass and snatches of raucous singing. The sad, sad pleasures of the young.

He looked out and up at the jewelled sky, tawny at its western margin where the lion city sprawled, and marshalled his sparse opinions on the after life. Wherever they were — Richard Scott and his fair daughter — up — down — around — beyond the blue horizon, they would know, surely? Wherever they were? Whoever they were? If ever they were? A pox on metaphysics! It had been done, and Lynch had done it, and Lynch knew it had been done, and that was enough for his philosophy. The car awoke at the first touch and he moved slowly out of the blue-rinsed emplacement, fastidiously rounding the unflinching worshippers, and halting at the exit, irresolute.

Drained and indecisive, he was still wide awake, the adrenalin decelerated but still coursing. Sleep was no answer to that kind of fatigue as well he knew.

His watch told him one o'clock. Too late for Datchet, even if he would have chanced it, decades too late. At the 'Crusader' the Glenlivet would have been lovingly locked away for the night, and in her behemoth of a bed, Biddy would be chasing fraudulent wholesalers down dream deep corridors.

But Up West, the clubs and casinos would be getting their second wind and grabbing their highwayman's portion of petrodollars. And, with any luck, Cappy Carpenter would be wassailing among his churls like a medieval baron.

The swinging city still swung, albeit creakily, and a little foolishly, in its middle years; rather like Lynch himself. He might as well swing with it.

THE END

Other titles in the
Linford Mystery Library:

THAT INFERNAL TRIANGLE

Mark Ashton

An aeroplane goes down in the notorious Bermuda Triangle and on board is an Englishman recently heavily insured. The suspicious insurance company calls in Dan Felsen, former RAF pilot turned private investigator. Dan soon runs into trouble, which makes him suspect the infernal triangle is being used as a front for a much more sinister reason for the disappearance. His search for clues leads him to the Bahamas, the Caribbean and into a hurricane before he resolves the mystery.

THE GUILTY WITNESSES

John Newton Chance

Jonathan Blake had become involved in finding out just who had stolen a precious statuette. A gang of amateurs had so clever a plot that they had attracted the attention of a group of international spies, who habitually used amateurs as guide dogs to secret places of treasure and other things. Then, of course, the amateurs were disposed of. Jonathan Blake found himself being shot at because the guide dogs had lost their way . . .